Delhi delights

About

Rudhir Prakash Sarma

Rudhir was born and brought up in the beautiful tea gardens of Assam & this infused in him a deep love for nature. After completing his graduation, he earned his daily bread as a PR executive. But it was only after he won a prize in a poetry contest organised by the Poetry Society of India in 2008 that he decided to take up writing seriously. After completing his Masters in Development Studies from IIT, Guwahati, he worked for some time in the development sector which was followed by a stint in the advertising sector. 'Delhi Delights' is his first novel. He is working on his second which is tentatively titled 'The last standoff at Saraighat'.

Delhi delights

Rudhir Prakash Sarma

Delhi delights (Novel)

Price in india : ₹ 150
Price out side india : $ 8

Published By : ***Redgrab books***
942, Mutthiganj, Allahabad, 211003
Website : www.redgrabbooks.com
E-mail : contact@redgrabbooks.com

ISBN : 978-93-87390-50-8
Printed at : Bhargava Press, Allahabad
Cover design : PixelR8 Studios
Edition : First, Paperback, September 2018

Dedicated To

A DEAR FRIEND WHO IS NO MORE

Life and death

Life can be as lovely as a rose,
or it can be as intense as a prose
But no matter how enticing, captivating or depressing it is,
Earthly existence, they say, is only a brief sojourn
Before the inescapable truth dawns upon us like self-realisation,
To take a stranglehold, never to let go
As life nears its lowest ebb and memories
become hazy in the approaching twilight,
Remorse sets in for all the past wrongdoings
that cannot be set right...

As a group of onlookers gather, a mixture of friends & foes,
A chosen few amongst them will shed tears
and still others will wax eloquence
about the numerous virtues of the departed,
Some real, some made up on the spur of the moment,
The lifeless body that lies within ear-shot
appears totally unperturbed,

The shroud forms a protective veil around the form,
Shielding it from more agony and harm,
Death finally makes us mortals lose our voice.

No need to grumble, no need to scorn
No need to ponder over what is to be worn
Death, they say, finally makes all our woes be gone.
No need to run after wealth and fame
No need to run after an unworthy aim
Want, want, want and want
They make us humans lose our sleep
Until, death at last chooses us as his keep.

Foreword

Does Delhi really delight? She might delight some and disappoint many. But that's not the point here. What matters is that Delhi attracts. Delhi is the dream destination of all politicians with high ambition. Delhi is the place for top bureaucrats to arrive at and prove their mettle in the labyrinths of the ministries and secretariats there. Delhi is also the direction in which creative artistes, painters, singers, and dancer would love to move in a bid to leave a mark on the national scenario.

But before all that, Delhi is also the destination of all those youngsters from across the country who have just passed their class X & XII and want to get higher education in a decent college or start getting coached for competitive exams. The protagonist of this book is also one such and through his travails and turmoil, the reader would get a first-hand feel of the events that keep happening after a youngster leaves the safety and security of his parental house and is exposed to the harsh realities of life.

This is one book that every youngster will find interesting because she or he may be preparing for a sojourn to Delhi for the reasons stated earlier. And for those, who have had this experience already, it would provide an opportunity to peruse through the pages and refresh the memories of their own times spent in the national capital. The members of every family that has kids who have been through these rigours of Delhi would also find the contents of the book very relevant and absorbing for them.

Rudhir Prakash Sarma's language is simple, lucid, and has the flow of a drawing room conversation. There is no place in the book where the reader would stumble or go back to see where he started from. It is this simplicity of narrative and almost real-life like depiction that would impel the reader to finish the book in one sitting.

Rajeev, the protagonist of the book, is all through in search of success but ultimately when he attains 'success', he is at a loss about what success is all about. This is one predicament that almost all of us encounter in life. The author has dealt with the matter with controlled and measured authority.

Success can be that tingle of excitement about what you do, sticking with what matters through hard times, living a life you can feel proud of in retrospect. But if the persons who you wanted to see and share your success have outlived your moment of glory, then all this success may feel like nothing at all.

'Delhi Delight' is one book that has dealt with a matter which is commonplace and not treated as a fiction as such ever before. It brings to life non-descript people and places and gets them imprinted in your thought process. A feel-good feeling! There are a host of happenings and incidents in between Rajeev's trip to Delhi and what leads him to other locations from there until he meets with 'success.' Every bit of that is true to life and stimulating. It's not for me to describe the story here. You go through the pages of 'Delhi Delights' and I tell you, you will be delighted.

Nurul Islam Laskar

(Former Consulting Editor, "The Sentinel"
& former Executive Editor, "Eastern Chronicle")

Acknowledgements

I dedicate this book to my late mother, who always encouraged me to chase my dreams. I thank my friends, Mr. Rupam Phukan & Mr. Mirza Arif Hazarika, my brother Robi & my wife Jahnvi for their words of encouragement & support.

I must thank my Dad who has always stood by me and supported me both mentally and financially when others seemed to have given up on me as a lost cause.

Finally, I offer my sincerest thanks to Nurul Laskar Sir for agreeing to pen the foreword.

Content

Delhi delights

CHAPTER-1

It was 7.00 am in the morning when Rajeev's cell phone started ringing. He woke up with a start when he saw the number on the screen. It was his dad calling from Punjab. Mr Ashok Arora, Rajeev's dad, had some good news for his son this time. He finally decided to let him go to Delhi for his higher studies. Rajeev heaved a sigh of relief because his parents were at first reluctant and were not in favour of sending their only son to a place far away from home for studies when so many good colleges were there in Guwahati, their own city. Rajeev was adamant and reassured his parents that he was old enough to take care of himself. Moreover, studying in a metro would open up a host of opportunities for him after the completion of his studies thus ensuring a better job for him, he reasoned. He had cleared his higher secondary exams with flying colours securing more than 75 percent marks and his parents were overjoyed with his performance and they did not want to be an obstacle in the path of their only son's progress. Mr Ashok owned a modest garment shop and earned just about enough to lead a decent life with his family. He had saved up some money to fund his son's higher education but even then he was worried whether he would be able to meet the needs of his son.

Rajeev immediately rang up Akhil, his close friend who too was planning to go to Delhi for higher studies. Akhil's dad was a rich businessman-a consumer electronics business magnate who owned a chain of outlets across Assam. Akhil was a mediocre student and the only reason he wanted to go to Delhi was to stay away from home and his mother. His parents were hardly on talking terms- his dad, Mr Gupta, remained too engrossed in business and his mother stayed at home criticising and talking ill of her husband for neglecting his family and spending most of his waking hours away from home. Akhil's relationship with his elder brother and sister was not very cordial; they remained busy with their own lives and were least bothered about what went on in their own house. Rajeev met Akhil at a small eating joint that was very popular with the young crowd and discussed about their journey plans and the admission procedure followed in some of the institutes that they were planning to approach for admission.

Mr Arora got busy in making the necessary arrangements for his son's journey. He was anxious about his son's well-being so far away from home even though he knew at the back of his mind and was confident that his son would not turn his back upon his studies and tread the forbidden path. The day finally came when Rajeev had to leave and Mr Arora along with his wife went to the railway station to see him off. Akhil had already reached the station in advance and was eagerly waiting for Rajeev to arrive. The train arrived at the platform at the appointed time and Rajeev after seeking the blessings of his parents bid goodbye to them and boarded the train that would take him to the city where he would be able to realise his long cherished dreams.

After journeying by train for two days they finally reached New Delhi Railway Station. The hustle and bustle outside & the people jostling for space made Rajeev feel uneasy. “Hey come on and stop staring”, Akhil called out impatiently. Rajeev looked around with a confused look. “Now come and help me get our luggage down from the upper berth”, implored Akhil. Rajeev shook his head and helped his friend with the luggage. Together they made their way to the pre-paid taxi stand and hired a taxi to South-Extension Part- 1. They decided to spend the night at a guest house in South Extension as a number of institutes shortlisted by them were in that area and it would be easier for them to locate them in the morning. Tired as they were, both of them could hardly sleep that night in anticipation of the things that were in store for them. Both of them woke up early the next morning and got ready for what would be a hectic day for them. They carefully arranged their mark sheets and certificates and after exchanging pleasantries with the guest house owner Mr Saxena, a tall burly fellow in his mid-fifties, went out looking for an eating joint to have their breakfast.

After looking around for some time they came to Gupta Chaiwale, a non-descript and poorly maintained tea stall but well-known in the Kotla Mubarakpur area for its bread-pakoras and samosas. Both of them ordered tea and stood at a corner near the shop. Guptaji, the owner could immediately make out that they were new in that area and were students looking to join some institute. After a small wait, tea was served to them and Rajeev and

Akhil quickly sipped their tea and dug into their samosas with gusto. After paying Guptaji, they went to an institute named International centre for management and computers which was located just a few blocks away. They went to the building which housed the administrative department of the institute. The outward appearance of the building was modest and as they stood outside and discussed about the reputation of the University the institute was affiliated to, Harilal, the watchman approached them, enquired about the purpose of their visit and led them to the reception where a couple of very well-dressed and beautiful looking ladies were handing out prospectus and forms to a group of boys and girls and explaining about the various courses on offer as well as the admission procedure. But the boys were busy ogling at the ladies and were least bothered about what they were talking about. Rajeev and Akhil glanced at each other and both could sense a wry smile form on each other's lips.

CHAPTER-2

They decided to wait for their turn and started leafing through the information brochures lying on the table. The wait lasted for about fifteen minutes and they waited for the boisterous group of boys and girls to exit the room before they made their move. The beautiful ladies at the counter smiled at them and politely enquired about the course they were interested in. Both of them were interested in pursuing BBA as their ultimate aim was to go for an MBA degree from a top-notch institute after completing their graduation. Being the flirt that he was, Akhil's eyes lit up when he got the opportunity to interact with the ladies and started behaving as if he had already made up his mind to join the institute. Seeing his behaviour and sensing the immediate need to quieten him, Rajeev gave Akhil a stern look and a poke in his ribs. Rajeev then took over and enquired about the institute's affiliation, course structure, exam schedule, placement opportunities and the fee structure. Students were granted admission on the basis of their performance in the board exams, interview and written test. But students securing above 70% in their board exams were granted spot admission.

After carefully noting down all the information that was required they thanked the ladies and came out. Next they decided to visit a few institutes located near Rohini and Janakpuri Market. They went to the pre-paid auto stand located near the adidas outlet at one end of the South Extension-I market and hired an auto. As it was admission time, the streets were full of students, many of them accompanied by their parents with anxious looks on their faces. Rajeev let out a sigh, and said a silent prayer to god to enable him to make the best possible decision regarding his future studies. The journey took them an hour and when they went in, the reception counter was already full of students anxiously leafing through their certificates and mark sheets over and over again while waiting for the results of the entrance test and interview. The staff manning the counter handed them a couple of forms each which they had to fill up and deposit along with a small amount as processing fee to be eligible for the written test.

At that moment a man came out from one of the classrooms and pasted a sheet of paper on the notice board containing the names of those students selected for the interview. There was joy on the faces of those who made it to the next round while sorrow was writ large on the faces of those who were unsuccessful. Rajeev turned his face away and took a deep breath. The next round of written test was arranged almost immediately after the results of the earlier batch of students were announced. Luckily both Rajeev and Akhil were allotted the same room. The questions were tricky and covered topics like general awareness, analytical reasoning, essay writing and grammar. Akhil attempted a few questions and sat chewing his nails and cursing himself under his breath for visiting that institute and waited impatiently for his friend to complete the test. Meanwhile, Rajeev was busy solving his paper and hardly had the time to look up and find out how his friend was faring. After an agonizing wait, the test was finally over and Akhil heaved a sigh of relief. He hurriedly submitted his answer-sheet and left the hall with Rajeev in hot pursuit.

Both of them went back to the reception counter and decided to wait till the results were announced. Rajeev knew that Akhil had not attempted most of the questions from the look on his face and scolded him for his careless attitude. But Akhil was least bothered as he hated exams. Moreover, as he had come to Delhi immediately after passing his board exams he was in no mood to even discuss about exams for the next few months. After some time the peon came and pasted another sheet of paper on the notice board. Rajeev walked over to check the list of selected students while Akhil followed him with a look of anger and frustration. As was expected, Rajeev managed to clear the test while Akhil failed to make the cut. After another wait, the admissions co-ordinator, a smartly dressed young lady, came out holding a register and pointing a red finger nail at Rajeev called out his name. Without looking at Akhil, he got up and moved quickly in the direction of the room where the interviews were taking place. The interview lasted for about fifteen minutes after which Rajeev went and collected the necessary forms required for completing the process of admission and left the building. Akhil was already waiting near the gate and without glancing at each other they got into an auto, which would take them to Janakpuri, their next stop. They did not utter a single word during this journey.

CHAPTER-3

"Bhai sahab, you have reached your destination", the auto rickshaw driver called out to Rajeev. Without saying a word Rajeev pulled out his purse and handed him the fare. Akhil had already got out and was making his entry on the visitor's register. Both of them went in after completing the necessary formalities. Akhil was impressed by the well-decorated interiors of the building and looked around to take in the sights and sounds while Rajeev was more concerned about the most important job at hand. After making the necessary enquiries he came to know that the admission tests for the next batch of applicants were to take place after a couple of days. He also enquired about the fee structure; hostel facilities and placement offers received by the previous batches and made a note of it. On their way back to the guest house both of them discussed about their day's work. While all three institutes visited by them had a fairly satisfactory record, the high fee structure was a cause of concern for Rajeev. As it was already late in the evening when they reached South Extension, both of them got down near Bengali Sweet House to have their dinner. The place was full of diners and the boys had to wait patiently before they could find a place to sit. Without poring over the menu card for too long, Rajeev immediately ordered rice, dal makhni, salad, raita and aloo zeera for himself while Akhil settled for a paneer masala dosa, moong ki dal ka halwa and a large glass of lassi to wash it all down with. By the time they finished their dinner it was already 9.30 in the evening. They settled the bill and walked hurriedly towards their guest house. Mr Saxena greeted them at the reception. Though the boys were tired and sleepy they greeted Saxena Ji warmly and took the room key from him after signing the register. They also filled him in on the day's happenings. After one final round of exchanging pleasantries they retired for the night in anticipation of another busy day ahead.

The next morning was bright and sunny and by the time the boys were up, Saxena Ji was busy taking orders for breakfast from the other occupants of the guest house. After making a round of his entire property and ensuring that the students who had put up as paying guests at his place were up and getting ready for their classes he knocked on the door of the room occupied by Rajeev and Akhil. Rajeev opened the door and greeted Saxena Ji who appeared to be in a cheerful mood. Although Rajeev was not sure, he guessed that the steady flow of guests was perhaps the reason for it. After all money makes the world go round, he thought. “The servant will come at eight in the morning accompanied by the sweeper and thoroughly clean your room. At what time would you like to have your breakfast? It would be easier for you if you have your breakfast here as you will then be able to head straight to the college; moreover food cooked outside is not very healthy, you don't want to fall sick, do you”? Saxena Ji went on. Rajeev was in no mood for a lengthy debate on this topic early in the morning and therefore nodded in approval. He ordered two omelettes; toast bread, butter and two large glasses of milk and went in to take a shower. Breakfast was already on the table by the time he finished taking his bath and got dressed.

Even as he applied a liberal coat of butter on his bread slices and tore into his omelette he spared some time to yell at his friend who was still fast asleep. Getting Akhil out of bed in the morning was a task fraught with grave risks as one not only had to put up with the choicest of abuses but also had to watch out for a flurry of vicious kicks that he let fly in all directions.

“Come on now, pour some more milk into my glass”,

yelled Akhil still looking sleepy after a shower even as he continued buttoning his shirt with one hand and combing his hair with the other. Rajeev chose not to counter his friend's rude behaviour and did as he was told as he knew that his friend was missing his pampered lifestyle back home.

CHAPTER-4

Once out on the street however his mood improved drastically. He started humming his favourite song and winked at Rajeev as he noticed a bevy of beautiful girls pass by. "The babes here know very well how to attract the male gaze, you know I have been to Mumbai once with my dad and I must say that while that place has quality, Delhi has quantity", Akhil whispered to Rajeev who knew what his friend was talking about but pretended as if he had not heard anything and instead looked around nervously as if he was trying to find out if someone had overheard his friend's comments. "Now come on dude, people here don't have the time or the inclination to listen to our conservation, and even if they do who cares. I feel it's time for you to shed that small-town mentality as it will do you no good here, you will have to be broad-minded and not let your lofty moral values determine every move that you make", Akhil remarked.

Both of them walked along silently till they reached the auto-stand. "What's our plan for the day"? Akhil called out to Rajeev who was lost in his own thoughts. "Well, hmm, our first stop for the day will be Delhi Business School, after that we will visit Rai Business School and our last stop for the day will be NDIM". "Ok buddy, let's get going, I guess we have another long and tiring day ahead", Akhil grumbled. The journey to DBS took quite a while and as they made their way to the office building the scene they witnessed inside the campus was similar to what they had witnessed the other day. There were too many students vying for a limited number of seats.

After waiting for their turn they were called in and as usual Rajeev took the lead in collecting the necessary details from the student counsellor while his friend sat almost motionless and disinterested staring at the ceiling. “What happened to you? I guess you didn't like the place. Otherwise I see no reason why you would have kept quiet”, Rajeev enquired on their way out. “Well, I must admit there were a few things that I wanted to ask but then I was wary of that poke in the ribs that you gave me the last time I showed some genuine interest. And since you did a fairly good job I chose not to interfere. Moreover, it does not really matter which institute I decide to join because it is up to you to decide. And I know you will make the right choice”, Akhil replied. “Well, well it would be great if you let me decide a few things and follow my advice on certain issues as it will help you keep away from trouble”, Rajeev replied with a smile as they set out for their next destination. The journey to Rai Business School took less than 20 minutes as it was also located on the busy Delhi-Mathura Road near Badarpur border and hardly a couple of kilometres away from the DBS campus. As they went inside they were impressed by the imposing corporate head office building that also housed the academic wing. It is known as the Espire Campus remarked Akhil as he glanced from one side to another. Let's check out this place and find out what are the courses on offer he called out again as he held the door open for Rajeev.

Once inside they were wondering whom they should approach when a cheerful and friendly looking young man approached them and led them to the student counsellor's office. “Madam is inside; you can collect all the information from her. By the way, I am Ravi Malik, BBA 2nd semester student”. Akhil introduced himself and his friend and a round of handshakes followed. “Thanks for your help Ravi, by the way, how did you know that we wanted to meet the counsellor”? Akhil remarked with a puzzled expression. “It is no rocket science buddy, since it is admission time most of the people who come here are students and when they come here, this is the first place they need to visit. Ok, then guys, I have to leave now, best of luck"! Ravi called out loudly, gave Rajeev a pat on his back and moved swiftly in the direction of a group of boys.

The two of them went inside the office and waited till they were told to sit. A young woman welcomed them and gave them a description about the courses on offer, the impressive list of full-time & part-time faculty members, teaching methodology followed, summer training opportunities and full-time placement offers received by some of the students. Rajeev was however more concerned about the fee structure and the frown on his brow became more visible when he was handed a slip containing the fee details. "You will no doubt agree that good education comes at a price and the investment that you make today for a good degree will give you handsome returns in the future. And we help students to secure bank loans besides offering scholarships to meritorious students coming from economically weaker sections of the society," the counsellor explained as if she could sense the cause of his ever expanding frown.

"Can I see your mark sheets if you don't mind", she continued trying to keep the conversation flowing and also to divert their attention to some other issues. "Well Rajeev, as you have done well in your board exams you are eligible for one of the many scholarships that are we are offering while your friend will have to pay the full amount as he does not meet our eligibility criteria for"..... "Its ok madam", Akhil interrupted even before she could finish, "I can manage without any kind of fee concession and I don't need any bank loan as well but does your institute provide accommodation to outstation candidates"? "Yes, why not, we provide excellent accommodation facilities to suit the needs of every student at our hostel campus in Faridabad known as the 'Meadows'. Students staying there also have the option of pursuing their studies at our meadows branch where the facilities are comparable to what the students enjoy over here".

"How far is that place from here? We would like to visit that campus as well before arriving at any decision", Akhil remarked as he signalled Rajeev to get up. "Its ok guys take your time. Hire a rickshaw and instruct the rickshaw puller to take you to Meadows, they normally charge ten rupees", the counsellor replied. "I would request you boys to leave your contact numbers with me so that I can keep in touch with you and assist you in completing the admission formalities", she continued. "Well, honestly speaking we haven't decided as yet which institute we are going to join and there are a few more places that we want to visit before taking a decision. But we will definitely get in touch with you should we require any further assistance", Rajeev replied politely as he made his way to the door.

"The rickshaws here are not very spacious", complained Akhil as he held on precariously to the hand grip while the rickshaw-puller continued pedalling as if he was preparing for the next leg of the Tour de France. The traffic movement was chaotic with those on the move jostling for space while the stationary ones were parked in a haphazard manner. But things improved and traffic movement became smooth once they crossed into Faridabad. As the rickshaw came to a halt right next to the main gate with a huge name plate in the background, the boys were spared the pain of asking for directions after a harrowing rickshaw ride and they went in straightaway without pausing for a moment. They had to cross two security check points and fill the visitor's register after explaining the purpose of their visit before they were escorted to one of the many multi-storied buildings in the campus that served as one of the boy's hostel. After checking out the place they were led to a row of single-storied blocks just adjacent to the basketball court. Even as Akhil & Rajeev went inside one of the few unoccupied rooms where renovation work was on in full swing, the man who accompanied them kept checking his watch every now and then and looking impatiently in the direction of the boys. “Boss, thoda jaldi kijiye, mujhe aap dono ko ek aur building mein leke jana hain”, he called out in a voice that had an unmistakable tinge of anger. Seeing him in such an agitated state, the boys started making their way out of the room even as their guide started walking briskly in the direction of a white-washed building situated behind the main boy's hostel building that they had been to a few minutes ago. “Iss wale hostel mein sirf non- air-conditioned, non- air-cooled kamre hain, aap log jaldi se dekh lijiye”, the man called out again. As all the rooms in that building were occupied the two of them saw no point in inspecting any of them and instead decided to take the long walk back to the main gate. “The main canteen is in the basement of the building to your left, while the cafeteria is located just opposite the warden's office”, the man pointed out without even bothering to look at them while he continued walking at the same brisk pace.

It took quite an effort from the boys to keep up with him and therefore they did not get the opportunity to stop and glance in the directions that he pointed at. But even then Akhil's curiosity was aroused by a building that was set apart from the ones they had been to. It was surrounded by high boundary walls and the entrance was guarded by a number of security personnel some of them even carrying firearms. As soon as the man came to a halt near the main gate Akhil paused for a moment, and after taking a few deep breaths went up to him and thanked him for the guided tour and handed him a fifty rupee note. “By the way, you did not take us to that building on your left; that place looks nice”. “Woh jagah aapke kaam ka nahin hain bhaiya, woh ladies hostel hain”, the man replied with a smile. “I see, well that explains the security around that place, the authorities have left nothing to chance in order to make the ladies feel safe, good for them,”, Akhil whispered to Rajeev even as they walked out after making their entry in the register and thanking the personnel manning the gate. “Well, now what! Let's go and find an eating joint or something, I am dying of hunger”, he continued, his whisper now turning into a growl.

The rickshaw had hardly come to a halt near the Haldiram's outlet when Akhil jumped out and hurried inside. “For a change, he did not grumble about the rickshaw ride this time”, Rajeev thought to himself with a smile as he handed the fare and followed his friend. In the meantime, Akhil had already found himself a place for two in a quiet corner and was busily leafing through the menu card almost tearing it in the process while the waiter looked on in bewilderment. They ordered chole bhatture, aloo-tiki and a plate each of rasmalai & gulab- jamun. After devouring the contents of his plate the smile returned to Akhil's face and as he waited for his friend to finish his meal, he took out the map and marked the place where Tughlakabad Institutional area was shown. “So that will be our last stop for the day, let's get going, what are we waiting for”, he called out impatiently the moment he saw Rajeev finish his meal.

“That's Batra Hospital Saxena ji told us about the other day, so I reckon we are not very far from our destination”, remarked Akhil still poring over the marks that he had made on the map. “I have heard a lot about their influential governing body and excellent industry interphase”, “It's interface, dear friend and by the way I was with you when you collected all that information from your friend so you need not repeat it all over again", interrupted Rajeev as the auto came to a halt outside the gate. "I guess, life is just a race to be the best in everything one does, look at our own predicament, we are supposed to join the best institute to pursue our studies and once that is done we have to line up outside the interview room along with the other job aspirants and land the best jobs on offer", Akhil grumbled. "Well, you are correct, but at the same time you need to understand that this race gives a sense of direction to our lives, it motivates us to strive harder, outperform the rest and be the best in our chosen field, and by the way we are here by choice as nobody forced us out of our homes, so cheer up and stop grumbling", Rajeev retorted.

After collecting the necessary details from the admissions office both of them went round the campus to have a look at the classrooms, computer centre and the library. "The library is quite impressive; it houses a number of useful journals along with a huge collection of books", Akhil remarked on their way back. "Let's call it a day man, I am dying to get under the shower and catch some shut eye. And we better decide which institute we are going to join as soon as possible, we cannot keep shuttling from one campus to another and just collect brochures & leaflets, moreover my dad will reach Delhi in a day or two and I have to let him know about our decision well in advance to enable him to make the necessary payments", Rajeev remarked with a huge yawn. "You are right; we also have to open our bank accounts and need to purchase a couple of mobile phones urgently, we cannot keep depending on Saxena Ji's landline number as we remain outdoors for most part of the day", Akhil reasoned.

The journey back to the guest house was smooth and

enjoyable. It was mid-July, and a thick cloud cover provided pedestrians as well as motorists some welcome respite from the scorching rays of the sun. A cool, pleasant breeze that gained intensity as the clouds engulfed the blue sky rapidly gave ample indications of the heavy downpour that was to follow. The neat rows of elegantly constructed houses in New Friends Colony were in stark contrast to the haphazard, unsystematic and jam-packed rows of houses in Kilokri and quite aptly depicted the difference between the filthy rich and the aspiring middle-class in India. "Will that gap be ever bridged, maybe after thirty or fifty years or considering the pace at which funds meant for the uplift of the underprivileged people in this country are siphoned off by the babus and the petty politicians in collusion with their higher-ups, maybe in another hundred years", Rajeev pondered. They passed the bhel puri wallas who did brisk business every evening selling their spicy, lip smacking preparations to many a hungry shopper, the fast food joints, the watch and jewellery stores and finally the Om Book shop before taking the right turn next to the chemist's shop. "Bas bhaiya, idhar side mein rok do", Akhil instructed as the auto came to a screeching halt just outside the gate.

Saxena ji who was relaxing on his reclining chair after his mid-day meal jumped up expecting some guests to walk in. He mostly preferred families although a major chunk of his clientele consisted of company executives. Looking after the needs of his six member family was not an easy task especially in a place like Delhi; and on top of that he was the only earning member in the house. But even then he was very straight forward when it came to his business dealings. He would not let out his place to young couples and people from Kashmir just to be on the safer side.

"Hey, what's wrong with you? What the hell are you

dreaming of"? Akhil roared in mock anger. "It's nothing", Rajeev replied as he got out clutching onto his carry bag and followed his friend inside. "You boys are back early today", Saxena ji said. "We didn't have to wait for too long anywhere today and that saved us a lot of time", Rajeev replied with a smile as he picked up the key and the newspaper lying on the counter and headed straight to his room.

CHAPTER-5

Chants of 'Om Namah Shivaya, Om Namah Shivaya, Jai Shiv Shankara Parameshwara......' followed by blowing of conch shells at the temple located at one end of H block announced that it was time for the evening aartis. Rajeev woke up feeling refreshed. His thoughts took him back to his home where everyone would wait for his mother to finish reciting her evening prayers before switching on the lights.

"Places of worship, prayer, religious ceremonies and the supernatural or the occult hold a special place in the lives of us Indians, they instil a sense of peace and calm in the minds of those weary souls who are overburdened by thoughts of material gain. It draws them to seek spiritual solace by introspecting into the meaning behind their own action's and their own existence. It provides them with that spark of inspiration, that strengthens their spiritual side just about enough to attain oneness with God, albeit for a fleeting moment, and brings true happiness, the kind, that one feels from the heart", Rajeev thought.

He got dressed and without waking up Akhil, who was still busy catching his forty winks, switched off the light and quietly closed the door behind him. An old man was sitting on the chair behind the cash counter reciting his prayers, eyes closed, hands folded in reverence in front of a small idol of Goddess Lakshmi, the Hindu goddess of wealth, kept in one corner of the glass cabinet. Rajeev quietly walked passed him and sat down on the sofa placed opposite to Saxena Ji's reclining chair. After his prayers were over, the old man sensed that someone was in the room and craning his neck looked in Rajeev's direction when he saw an unknown face.

Rajeev got up and folding his hands into a neat

Namaste introduced himself. “So you are Rajeev, my son told me about you”, the old man replied with a smile. “Where is your friend? Hope you guys are enjoying your stay in Delhi aren't you? By the way, I am Madan Mohan Saxena, I was at my youngest son's place in Ghaziabad otherwise you would have been seen me much earlier. I normally stay upstairs but like to spend most of my waking hours downstairs. My son has gone out to the tourism department's office and I am looking after this place”, the old man went on. “I spent three days in Assam some years ago, during the elections doing election duty”, Dadaji said. “It's a nice place, full of greenery, but the centre allotted to us was in an insurgency infested area somewhere in Goalpara, we camped in a high school and a posse of armed policemen and CRPF personnel were deputed to keep us safe, but at the dead of the night we heard the sound of gunshots and were scared like anything”, Dadaji said. “The security personnel returned the fire, luckily none was killed, but one policeman sustained minor injuries, later someone told me that they were the disgruntled local youths, who had formed an armed outfit to liberate their state from the so-called illegal occupation by the imperialist Indian forces. We were badly shaken by the incident but there was no turning back until our job was done. News of the incident spread like wildfire and as a result the voter turnout on the day of the polls was abysmally low as most of the people preferred to stay indoors than come out and face the ire of the militants who had issued a terse warning to the people to boycott the polls. There was no long queue outside and the few people who turned up were outnumbered by the security personnel present and by five in the evening only about thirty percent of the voters had exercised their franchise. I, along with three of my colleagues was driven to Guwahati early in the morning the next day from where we took the afternoon flight back to Delhi. And boy o boy!

Wasn't I glad to be able to return home; those three days spent there seemed almost like an eternity. Hope the situation is better now", Dadaji said with a sigh, probably tired after speaking for so long.

"There is no improvement; on the contrary things have deteriorated owing largely to the stand taken by the local politicians, who want to keep insurgency alive in the North East in order to usurp the funds that the Centre keeps doling out in generous quantities in the name of weeding out these anti-social elements and taking up developmental works", replied Rajeev with a downcast countenance. "And to make matters worse, those so-called crusaders fighting for the rights of the indigenous people have taken shelter in neighbouring Bangladesh owing to the counter-insurgency operations launched by the government. They have now become pawns in the hands of Islamic fanatics working with the tacit support of a section of the politicians and the intelligence agencies of that country who are encouraging mass illegal immigration into Assam in general and the North East in particular besides parts of West Bengal, Bihar & Jharkhand. The leaders have turned a blind eye to this problem owing to vote-bank politics and very soon these land-hungry, uncouth & filthy immigrants emboldened by such gracious patronage will start attacking the locals in order to grab their land and harass their women thereby causing communal unrest while our saviours who have taken up arms vowing to fight for our rights would only be able to watch helplessly as their fellow brethren are reduced to second-class citizens in their own land, said Rajeev", his voice trembling with anger. "Unfortunately that is not the case only with Assam, the rest of India is also facing the same problem owing to the lack of far-sightedness of our politicians. I feel that we are also to be blamed for this problem. Most of us lack political consciousness and do not vote when we get the opportunity to elect the right people. As a result the shrewd politicians are pampering these immigrants by doling out voter cards, free electricity, free ration and what not to them to remain in power. And as they don't demand roads, bridges, schools and more jobs like us, the leaders have the liberty to do whatever they want to with the funds at their disposal", Dadaji said. Rajeev got up and after excusing himself decided to take a walk outside. He needed some fresh air to lift his spirits after such a serious talk. He hated the feeling of powerlessness that he felt whenever he discussed such issues and longed for the day when he would be able to contribute something significant to matters close to his heart.

"Hey! What's up? 'Akhil said as he crept up from behind and placed his shoulder round his friend's neck. I was listening to your conversation with the old man, I agree with your views but what is the use of getting agitated over such issues when you can't do much, so cheer up man", Akhil said. "Let's take a walk in the market, the bright lights & the sight of the dazzling beauties will make you feel better", he continued.

"Don't know what to do next, my parents want me to join the best institute but good education comes at a hefty price these days and I know my dad won't be able to arrange that kind of money", Rajeev remarked with a frown on his face. "Why do you worry about finances? If required, I am there to help you out", Akhil said. "I cannot borrow money from you. If I cannot afford the admission fees then how am I going to complete my studies here? Besides, how am I going to repay you"? Rajeev questioned. "Don't worry dear, I am not running away anywhere anytime soon and about the repayment part, well you can start worrying about that once you get a job", Akhil responded.

"Anyway your dad will be here tomorrow won't he?

You needn't be so anxious, everything will be alright", Akhil said with a smile. Finding some solace in the words of his friend, Rajeev accompanied him to the park with the remarkably well-maintained lawns located next to Chawlaji's Restaurant for a leisurely stroll. Although the park was located next to a Mughal era tomb, a group of young kids running around the place playing hide and seek at that late hour in the evening made it amply clear that there was nothing sinister to it.

"So what do you want to have for dinner", Akhil asked lightly tapping Rajeev on his shoulder. "Hmm, err, anything you like, but please order some raita or dahi for me", Rajeev replied.

"Hey, try the paneer butter masala, its yummy" said Akhil. "No thanks, I have had enough, pass me the water bottle, you have your food while I take a walk outside", Rajeev said. "Ok, but don't be late", replied Akhil without looking up even as he greedily wolfed down a spoonful of gajar halwa. Rajeev was planning to walk up to the Mother Dairy outlet and purchase a pouch of flavoured milk when through the corner of his eye he saw Saxena Ji standing outside the door and waving at him. His footsteps quickened as he saw the urgency in the manner in which the burly man was gesturing at him and by the time he reached the door he was already gasping for breath. "It's a phone-call from your dad", Saxena Ji said. "Hello son, how are you? I have reached Patna and will be in Delhi by tomorrow evening", Mr Arora said as soon as Rajeev picked up the receiver. "Had you dinner, dad"? Rajeev questioned. "Yes. Now tell me how far your place is from the station"? Mr Arora asked.

CHAPTER-6

"It took us forty-five minutes that day", Rajeev said. "And listen son, you don't have to come to the station to receive me, I will manage it on my own and will contact you in case of any difficulty", Mr Arora said sternly. "Good Night dad, try to have a good night's sleep and see you tomorrow", Rajeev replied.

"So your dad will be here tomorrow", Saxena said. "You should book a room for him if he is planning to stay for a few days", he continued. Rajeev nodded his head but refrained from making any comment. "Good Night uncle", Akhil said as he took a few steps in the direction of his room waiting for his friend to follow. Rajeev followed knowing well that the portly man was feeling slighted as he did not get a proper reply to his query. "Don't think too much about what he said, ever since we landed up here I have lost count of the number of times he has talked about his list of clients and his good contacts", Akhil said angrily. "750 per day for the luxury and 550 per day for the economy room", mocked Akhil mimicking the voice of Saxena ji. "I am switching off the lights, let's go to sleep. We have to wake up early tomorrow and arrange our clothes & other items properly, our room is in a mess", said Akhil.

For a change, Akhil was the one who woke up early the next morning and after a light breakfast got busy in cleaning up the almirah where his clothes were lying in a heap. "What a surprise? You are actually trying to tidy up the room, unbelievable", Rajeev said as he got up rubbing his eyes in bewilderment. "Now cut the crap man. I could do with some help from you so if you are not planning to go out anywhere please go and brush your teeth and have your breakfast and after that if you feel like joining me you are most welcome", Akhil said. The clock had struck eleven by the time they had finished and both of them were admiring their good work and thanking each other when they heard a car come to a halt followed by the sound of heavy footsteps walking up to the reception.

"Saxena ji Namaste,kya haal chaal hain aapke? Kuch mehmanoko leke aayan hoon", a man said in a gruff voice. "Yeh log kahan se aayen hain"? Saxena Ji said without any change of expression. "Afghani hain, treatment ke liya aayen hain", the man said in a muted tone as two burly men made their way towards the counter, one supporting himself on crutches and the other pulling along two huge suitcases. "Pehle Dekh leta hoon, kis kaam se aaye hain phir room ke bare mein baat karenge", Saxena Ji said in a very matter-of-fact manner. "I am Nasir Mohammad and he is Kasem Mohammad Nur, my father. We have come from Kandahar to consult a doctor at the AIIMS. My dad sustained a splinter injury during a brutal terror attack in Kabul and the doctors there advised us to consult a specialist here", the man pulling the suitcases said. "May I see your passports if you don't mind? You will have to give me photocopies so that I can deposit the same at the Tourist registration office", Saxena Ji said. "In addition to that there are two rules, consuming alcoholic drinks and indulging in any form of objectionable behaviour is strictly prohibited here", Saxena Ji said. The two Afghans nodded their heads in unison without replying.

CHAPTER-7

"Rent is 750 per day for the luxury and 550 for the economy; you may inspect the rooms if you feel like", Saxena Ji spoke again at the same time motioning to Chandra, the domestic help who also doubled up as the bell-boy to take the key from him and lead the guests to their room. Nasir followed him and after his return whispered something into the ear of his father who shook his head violently. "The room is clean and spacious but as we are planning to stay for a long duration we would request you to offer us some discount", Nasir said. "Normally, our rates are fixed but for you I can reduce the tariff to 700 per day", Saxena Ji said. "No Sir, you not understanding, long stay means big income for you, so we need more discounts", Kasem spoke for the first time in broken English with a big frown on his face, his crutches barely retaining its grip on the floor as he moved forward.

"I am sorry, I can offer you no more discounts, I have to take care of my other expenses incurred in running this place and make some profit as well", Saxena Ji said politely even though he was taken aback by the rude manner in which Kasem spoke. "No, you are not trying to understand, today 750, tomorrow 650, day after 550, then 450 like that", Kasem spoke again. "We are not running a Dharamshala here, I think you have come to the wrong place, I already let you know my final offer, if that is not acceptable to you then you are free to leave", Saxena Ji said running out of patience. "No you do not understand, today 750, tomorrow 650....." Kasem began again but was cut short by Saxena Ji who got up from his chair. "Stop it, no use arguing unnecessarily, you are wasting my time", he hissed angrily as he went near the taxi-driver. "From where have you brought these people behenchod, take them away before I lose my cool", he continued in a menacing tone.

"Decide quickly Sir, or else we will leave", Nasir spoke making one last ditch attempt to try and make him change his mind. "I have already made things very clear to you so please leave immediately", Saxena Ji said tersely pointing towards the door. As the three of them left, Saxena Ji saw Rajeev and Akhil standing near the corridor and motioned to them to join him in the lobby. "I had a tough time dealing with a couple of Afghan guys. I guess every business has its positive and negative sides. I think your dad will be here soon", he said pointing a finger in Rajeev's direction. Rajeev nodded his head in agreement. Almost at the same moment an auto came to a halt near the gate. Rajeev rushed out when he saw his dad get out with a suitcase. Akhil held the door open for them while Saxena ji folded his hands into a neat Namaste as Mr Arora made his way into the lobby and sat down on the sofa. "So how was your trip"? Saxena Ji asked. He picked up the intercom and told Chandra to get four cups of tea and some biscuits. "I guess you have come for your son's admission", Saxena Ji continued the conversation. "Yes, I am here for a couple of days and would like to complete all formalities by tomorrow. I need a room; a simple one would suit me just fine. How much do I have to pay you"? Mr Arora spoke for the first time.

CHAPTER-8

After making the necessary payments and signing on the guest register, Mr Arora headed straight to his room. "Both of you come to my room after a few minutes, I need to discuss tomorrow's program with you guys", he said nodding in the direction of the two boys. Mr Arora had already ordered tea and snacks when Rajeev & Akhil walked into the room. "So what have you guys decided"? Mr Arora asked. "Well dad I want you to visit the institute tomorrow and if you like what you see we will take it further", Rajeev spoke. "I told both of you to choose a good institute. Why do you want me to decide for you? Since you two have decided to pursue your studies here you will also have to learn to take some important decisions yourself", Mr Arora said. The boys nodded their heads quietly.

After a brief wait the boys were led into the office where they were greeted by the two beautiful young ladies once again. Mr Arora was only concerned about the credibility of the institute but he trusted the judgement of his son. "So how much money do I have to pay now son"? Mr Arora asked. Rajeev did a quick calculation. "Rupees forty thousand dad for the first semester", Rajeev said. "When will the classes start"? Mr Arora asked the admissions-in-charge even as he collected the money receipts. "Classes will start from mid-July and the study-material would be distributed by the end of this month sir", the lady replied after she had finished counting the cash for a second time and putting it away in the locker.

The two boys congratulated each other. "Ok, now what"? Mr Arora asked. "I am feeling hungry. What was the name of that restaurant you were talking about yesterday"? He continued. "Kent's Fast Food", Akhil quipped. Any talk about food always made him hungry. Akhil ordered a maha burger with French fries and a glass of fruit juice while Rajeev and his dad settled for a paneer burger and a cup of coffee each.

"Arora Ji, the servant has just finished cleaning your room", Saxena Ji said as he handed over the key to Rajeev. "So boys, now that you have got admission I would want you to concentrate on your studies right from day one", Mr Arora said as soon as they got inside the room. The boys nodded their heads in unison. "I need some rest. Wake me up after a couple of hours", he continued when he saw them walking towards the door.

"Have some Prasad dad", Rajeev said as soon as he saw his dad standing in the corridor. "I told you to wake me up before going out", Mr Arora said. "We thought you were tired uncle and so you decided to let you rest", Akhil said.

"It's okay for today but make sure to take me along when you go out in the evening tomorrow. I too want to visit the temple", Mr Arora said with a smile.

"Want to go out for a cup of coffee"? Rajeev asked after looking at his watch. "No thanks. Saxena ji brought me tea and snacks sometime ago", Mr Arora replied. "He has gone out with his wife to Chandni Chowk to attend a birthday party", Mr Arora continued as he went inside his room.

"Hey Rajeev, your mom wants to speak to you", Mr Arora called out. Rajeev hurried inside. "Hello mom. How are you"? I am fine he said. "I am doing good son. Hope you are enjoying your stay in Delhi. Please take good care of your health. How is Akhil"? Rajeev's mom replied. "The weather here is awful but I am getting used to it. Akhil is doing well too mom", Rajeev replied. "Tell Akhil to attend classes regularly", his mom said. "Mom, why don't you have a word with him", Rajeev said and passed the phone to his friend. "How are you Akhil beta"?

Mrs Arora asked. “Fine Aunty”, Akhil replied. “Your dad called me up yesterday son. He is worried about your future. So Study hard and make him proud. And both of you always stick together like good friends”, Mrs Arora said. “Okay Aunty”, Akhil said and handed the phone back to Mr Arora. “Don't worry Kavita, Saxena ji is a good man. He will take good care of the boys. Take care and good night”, Mr Arora said and disconnected the call.

“Are you planning to go out for dinner”? Mr Arora asked Rajeev. “No dad”, Rajeev shook his head. “Would it be okay if I order poori, subji and raita for dinner”? Mr Arora asked. The boys nodded in agreement.

CHAPTER-9

"Son, I am going out for a walk. Get up and be ready for breakfast before my return", Mr Arora said before closing the door behind him. Rajeev got up and went to his room. Akhil was still fast asleep. "Akhil wake up", Rajeev said after tapping lightly on his shoulders. Rajeev picked up two buckets and headed straight to the bathroom. "Good morning Rajeev. Fill your buckets quickly as water supply has become very erratic these days", Saxena ji said even as he hurriedly watered the potted plants. "Bathing early in the morning has its advantages. One gets to use a clean toilet", Saxena ji said while Rajeev wondered what the other advantages could be.

"Come on Akhil, hurry up. We are waiting for you", Rajeev yelled. "I will join you in five minutes", Akhil replied even as he poured another mug of water over his body. "Son, I have made a list of the items you would require. Go through it and add if anything is missing", Mr Arora said to Rajeev post breakfast. "Do you want to come along Akhil"? Rajeev asked as he stepped out of the room with his dad. "Sure", he said and followed them outside.

"This place is so crowded. It reminds me of Fancy Bazar back home", Akhil said while negotiating a crowded lane in Kotla Market. They continued walking till they came to a shop selling utensils and plastic items. "Rajeev, let's go inside. I think we better purchase a large container to store water to last you a couple of days", Mr Arora said. "How much does this one cost"? He asked eyeing a red and blue container. "Six hundred", the shopkeeper said without getting up from his chair. "Three hundred", Mr Arora countered. "No way bhaisaheb, pay five hundred", the shopkeeper said. "Three hundred leave it or take it", Mr Arora said and pretended as if he would walk out from the shop. The old trick worked. "Okay three hundred it is", the shopkeeper said. "Sonu please pack the container", the shopkeeper said and a young boy came running with a piece of cloth and after wiping the dust off it tied it neatly with a rope using several layers of newspaper. "Boys, get back to the hostel with this container. I will buy the rest of the items and join you for lunch", Mr Arora said. "Dad, Saxena ji enquired whether you want to go sight-seeing"? Rajeev asked after his dad returned. "No son, this is my tenth visit to Delhi. Moreover, I don't feel like going out anywhere in this heat", Mr Arora replied. "Have you spoken to Saxena ji about changing your rooms? Shift immediately if the hostel rooms are ready otherwise footing your accommodation bills would become a tall order for me", Mr Arora said. "At what time are you leaving tomorrow dad"? Rajeev enquired. "I am leaving by the 2424 Dibrugarh Rajdhani Express at 2.00 pm", Mr Arora replied. There was a knock on the door. "Uncle Ji chai", the servant said and placed a cup of tea and a few bread slices on the table. "Tell uncle that my dad wants to meet him", Rajeev told him as he left the room. "Uncle will come downstairs at 10 am after breakfast", the servant whose name was Chandra said. "Okay, we will wait for him", Rajeev said.

CHAPTER-10

Mr Arora was reading the morning newspaper when Saxena ji turned up with his dad. "Good morning Arora ji! I am going out to attend a hearing with my dad", Saxena ji said. "Since I am leaving tomorrow, I wanted to discuss about my son's hostel accommodation with you", Mr Arora said. "I will be back by 12 noon. So if it's okay with you we can discuss after my return", Saxena ji offered. "Will wait for you then and all the best for that hearing", Mr Arora replied. "So there goes that fellow again, after making us wait for so long", Mr Arora said in anger. "I am going to catch some shut eye. You guys go and have your lunch. I am not hungry", he continued. The boys looked at each other not knowing what to say.

Mr Arora was awakened by the sounds of footsteps and the Saxena father and son duo arguing loudly. "So you are back Saxena ji", Mr Arora said determined not to let him slip away once again. "Are the hostel rooms ready"? He asked. "Yes, they are. The workers are cleaning the rooms and the boys can move in by today evening", Saxena ji said even as he wiped off beads of sweat from his face. "What about the room rent and other charges"? Mr Arora asked. "Charges are Rupees Twenty five hundred per bed on a twin sharing basis and canteen charges will be Rupees Fourteen hundred per month which will include breakfast, lunch and dinner on all days of the week except Sundays", Saxena ji elaborated. "During winter, we provide warm water for bathing at a nominal cost of Five Rupees per bucket", he added. "All boarders have to pay two month's rent in advance as security deposit which is adjusted against monthly rent if someone wishes to leave the hostel with prior notice. And finally, there is a canteen maintenance charge of Rupees four hundred per year", he continued. "Okay, I will make the payment in the evening", Mr Arora said and walked back to his room.

"There goes the last one", Akhil said as he literally hurled his suitcase inside the room allotted to him and Rajeev. "It's just like being dumped on the pavement. How can this room accommodate two persons"? Akhil grumbled. "Stop complaining now. Do you remember the kind of money we had to shell out for spending a few days and nights in air-conditioned comfort"? Rajeev said. "Things will fall into place after a few days, trust me", Rajeev continued. "Boys have you finished moving your luggage? If so, then please join me for dinner", Mr Arora said. The boys hurried inside. As the three of them sat down to eat they hardly looked at each other and none uttered even a single word. "Keep this with you", Mr Arora said handing Rajeev an envelope containing crisp five hundred rupee notes. "Spend it wisely. This should last you a couple of months", he continued. Just then, a car came to a screeching halt outside which was followed by a knock on the door. "Arora Ji, the taxi has arrived", Saxena Ji called out. Mr Arora looked back in the direction of the boys, slightly thumped Rajeev's shoulder and went out after picking up his luggage.

Rajeev stood still for some time even as the taxi carrying his dad turned left and was soon out of sight. It was now that he realised what his dad meant when he said 'you would be on your own now'. He knew he would miss the comforting presence of his parents near him for the first time in his life.

CHAPTER-11

"I say Akhil, let's go and find out from the Director when our classes are starting from. They said that classes will start from the 14th July without fail but today is 25th", said Rajeev pacing around his room anxiously. "Relax Rajeev, don't get so worked up. They must be having some issues. Let them get back to us", Akhil replied casually. "Okay so you aren't going then"? Rajeev glared at Akhil as he began to walk out of the room. "Wait dude. We are in this together remember. Let's go", Akhil said.

At the institute, the now familiar faces of Brijesh and Gurudev bhaiya greeted them. "We would like to meet the Director", Rajeev said. "Sorry, Director Sahab is out of station. May I know the purpose of your visit"? Gurudev asked. "We were just wondering when our classes are going to start", Akhil quipped. "Don't worry; there is good news for you guys. The Director has issued instructions that classes should start without fail by the 30th. There were some issues which have been sorted out, so now you guys can breathe easy", Gurudev spoke reassuringly. "See, I told you didn't I that everything will be fine", Akhil said as the boys began their walk back to their hostel.

"Come on, wake up Akhil, today is the first day of college and I don't want us to be late", Rajeev said almost pulling Akhil out of bed. "Okay, okay, I can get up myself. It looks like you are too eager to hog the limelight on the very fast day just like you did in school don't you"? Akhil said throwing his hands up in protest. "Thanks Chandra", Akhil said to the servant boy after finishing his breakfast as the two boys set out for their classes.

The hustle & bustle all around was unmistakable as they made their way into the building. There were some boys and girls with nervousness writ large on their faces as they went about looking for their classrooms and at the same time were anxious to avoid the prying eyes of their seniors. The classroom allotted to the BBA first semester batch was located in the basement and as the boys went inside and took their seats, a handful of their classmates were already busy in making small-talk.

“Let's occupy those back seats on the right”, Akhil said as he stood to one side and allowed Rajeev to pass by. “Are you going out again”? Rajeev asked. Akhil shook his head instead of replying as he walked in the direction of the small group that was busy in a conversation. “Hi miss, I am Akhil”, he said to a lady in a pink dress and high-heels. “Jyotika here”, she replied and shook hands with a look which made it amply clear that she was a confident young woman. “So are you from these parts”? She asked.

“By the way, I am from Jammu but have been living here since the last four years”, she added. “I see. Well, I am from Assam, the remote north-east as people here like to call it”, Akhil replied with a smile. Just then, a well-dressed man walked in. “Good morning students, I am Professor Arvind Mohan and will be teaching you financial accounting during the first semester. Classes are cancelled for today, but I want you all to be present in the auditorium for the welcome address by the Dean”, he stated.

“You know what, instead of this boring speech stuff, why don't they allow the seniors to come and rag us”, Akhil said as they made their way to the hall. “It would have been so much fun”, he added. “And I say, why don't you keep your bloody ideas to yourself and just keep moving”, Rajeev replied with a nudge to Akhil's back as if to emphasize his point.

“Phew! That was some welcome address”, Akhil remarked on their way back. “I wonder how I am going to sit through those countless lectures if I can't stand an hour long speech", he added. "Undoubtedly an issue that needs your immediate attention", Rajeev nodded even as Akhil clenched his fist in disgust. "Hey! I can see a number of people standing near the gate and talking to Saxena ji", Akhil said. "I guess today is his lucky day, and finally the hostel is going to be fully occupied", Rajeev replied.

"Hello', Rajeev answered the call. His mother was at the other end. 'Don't worry Ma, everything is fine. Our classes are starting from tomorrow. Convey my regards to Dad. Love you Ma", he ended the call. "Boys, if you are not busy would you mind coming out for a couple of minutes", Saxena ji called. "Right away, uncle", both boys spoke at once. "I want you to meet Sameer Garg, senior most boarder of this hostel. He will tell you how I run this place", Saxena ji said.

"And these two boys have moved in today. One is Sahil Khan and the other is Vinit Sharma", he added. "I hope you guys will get along nicely", he continued even as he got up and motioned something with his hands to Sameer before going upstairs. "Bhaiya, how long have you been here"? Rajeev asked. "Since the last couple of years", he replied. "And I am glad that you guys have moved in as otherwise this place gets quite lonely in the evenings", he added with a smile.

"By the way, I am pursuing a course in fashion management at IIFT", Sameer said. "Is that so? Even I have enrolled in their fashion management programme. I hope I will get a job after completion", Vinit spoke with an unmistakable hint of excitement in his voice.

CHAPTER-12

"That will depend on how well you cope with your studies and acquire the desired skills", Sameer replied with a look that showed even he was unsure about getting a job. "Alright, what about the other three of you here"? He continued determined to change the topic of discussion. "Both of us have joined the BBA programme at IMC", Rajeev said pointing at himself and Akhil.

"Great, finally I have found someone from the same institute. So how was day one at the institute"? Sahil asked. "Nothing much happened today barring a boring speech, but I have a feeling that major excitement is in store", Akhil spoke with a mischievous glint in his eyes. "Dinner is ready. Please come upstairs with your plates", Chandra announced and left quickly. "The malai kofta and bitter gourd do not click as a combination", Sahil remarked as he pushed his plate aside. "I agree but do we have a choice", Akhil replied. "Let's go out for a walk. It will help cheer up the grumpy looking faces", Rajeev said after finishing his meal in a leisurely fashion. "Seriously guys, we will have to make some other arrangement if the quality of food does not improve", Sahil said. "Let's not be so impatient, friend. You will get used to it", Rajeev replied. "Let's see, good night guys", Sahil said. "We have a busy day ahead. Get a good night's sleep", Akhil replied back.

"Come let's go, it's already 9.15", Rajeev said impatiently looking at his watch. "Let Sahil come. He will feel bad if we walk away without him", Akhil said. "Sorry, I kept you waiting", Sahil apologised. "No big deal. Let's move", Akhil said diplomatically. "That's my class and your class is next to mine. Isn't it great? I won't be missing you guys so much now", Sahil said as he entered his class.

Akhil went in ahead of Rajeev and surveyed the classroom. The attendance was better than the previous day. And from the corner of his eye he could see Jyotika entering the class with her friend. “Hi Jyotika”, he called out. “Hello Akhil”, she replied with a smile.

Exactly at 9.30 am, Professor Arvind walked in. “Students, I see a significant increase in attendance compared to yesterday. Good for you all”, he said. “Since the class tests and end-semester exams are accorded almost equal weightage here, you guys will have to be punctual and studious to ensure good grades. I hope, I have made myself amply clear”, the Professor said with a smile. “Yes Sir”, the students said in unison. “All right, let's start with a round of introduction then”, Professor Arvind said.

“Arvind and Aman Sirs are quite friendly. But I can't say the same about Monika Madam and the others. In fact, their faces look scarier than the books we are carrying”; Akhil said tapping the books slightly. “Don't worry man. How can you form an opinion on the very fast day? Give them a fair chance”, Rajeev said with a laugh. “What is the name of the girl you were talking to”, Rajeev continued. “Jyotika Kohli. She is a beauty, isn't she”? Akhil replied his eyes lighting up. “You know I am planning to take her out for lunch tomorrow”, Akhil added. “Don't you think that would be a bit too soon”? Rajeev questioned. “Okay then, I will delay it by a few days. The weekend would be fine I guess”, Akhil said. “Hmm, at least you seem to have some positive intent on this issue”, Rajeev remarked with a mischievous smile. “Hey guys, sorry I couldn't join you for lunch. You know there are quite a few guys from your place in my class”, Sahil said. “We are planning to go out in the evening. Why don't you join us”? Akhil said. “Okay sure”, Sahil said.

“How far are we going”? Rajeev asked as soon as Akhil and Sahil joined him outside the gate. “Well, let's go to the park in Kidwai Nagar. It is spacious and not very crowded at this time in the evening”, Akhil said after a thought. “Fine, let's go, but I only hope the place is not very far. Walking long distances in this heat is not a pleasing thought”, Sahil said.

“You know I was thinking about the food. I have found a place where the food is delicious and affordable and they do home delivery as well. So I want you guys to try out this place tonight”, he added. “You two go ahead if you like. The hostel food is okay for me”, Rajeev replied. “Oh, come on man! At least join us for tonight”, Sahil said raising his hand in protest. “If you want, I can inform Saxena ji not to prepare dinner for us today”? He volunteered. “And what would be the excuse”? Rajeev asked. “I will say that we are going to eat outside. And even if I don't call what's the big deal? We are paying him anyway. I will tell Chandra to serve us small helpings, that's it”, Sahil said. “Namaste, Chawla ji, as you can see, I have brought my friend's along tonight. So don't disappoint me”, Sahil said with a wink as soon as he entered a congested and dull-looking eating joint by the road-side.

“We will have roti, paneer bhujia, dal makhni and aloo jeera”, he yelled. As the boys began tearing into their rotis, Chawla ji walked up to them with three glasses of lassi. “That's complimentary since you all have come here for the first time”, he said pointing at Rajeev and Akhil and left. “Thanks Uncle”, Sahil said.

CHAPTER-13

"Rajeev, can you accompany me to the library after class today"? Akhil asked. "Sure thing dude, but I find it strange that you have suddenly developed such a fondness for books", Rajeev replied as they walked past the temple on their way to class. "You see, life is all about making the right adjustments at the right time", Akhil said. "We'll see about that", Rajeev replied.

"Let's go", Akhil said as soon as classes were over. "There is a slight change in plans. I think you have not been to the roof-top cafe, have you? It's a nice place for spending some time with friends", he continued as he led the way. "But you told me", Rajeev tried to protest but was cut short by Akhil who motioned him to keep quiet. "Sorry, I made you wait for too long. But why didn't you attend the last class", Akhil said to someone as he walked into the cafe with Rajeev some distance behind him. "By the way, he is my best buddy Rajeev, also from Guwahati", Akhil said as Rajeev suddenly stood face to face with Jyotika for the first time. "Hi Rajeev, guys she is Tulika Subramanian", Jyotika replied as she introduced her friend to the boys.

"Well Akhil, I just felt like taking a break. Attending four to five consecutive classes is so boring", she added. As soon as they found themselves a nice place in the corner, Akhil signalled to a waiter to take their orders. "Get us French fries, sandwiches and a cup of coffee each", Akhil placed the order after consulting the others. "So Tulika, you are like my friend I guess. Don't speak too much, do you"? Akhil asked. "I like listening to other people speak", she replied in a voice that had that typical South-Indian accent. "So how you guys did become such close friends? I mean you seem to be poles apart", Tulika asked. “Well that is a long story but I guess you will be able to get a fair idea just by observing us”, Akhil replied.

“And by the way, Rajeev is quite a charmer once he gets over his initial hesitation. Just give him a chance”, Akhil added with a naughty smile which earned him an angry poke on his elbow from Rajeev. Tulika's mobile beeped. “Sorry guys got to go. My dad is here to pick me up”, she said as she hurriedly picked up her belongings and left. “Jyotika, what are you doing tomorrow”, Akhil asked suddenly as Rajeev looked nervously away from the table. “Nothing much, why”? She replied. “Would you like to join me for lunch”? Akhil asked with an abruptness that even stunned the lady. “Okay, but it has to be a place nearby. I want to relax and catch up with my studies during holidays”, she replied. “Are you joining us, Rajeev”? She asked. “Umm no, he fasts on Saturdays”, came the reply from Akhil even before Rajeev could open his mouth. “Okay then, shall we leave”? Akhil asked as he stood up. “I have already settled the bill”, he said when he saw Jyotika rummaging through her bag.

CHAPTER-14

"So you are the large-hearted guy over here", Jyotika said with a smile. "Yes occasionally, when I am in the company of good friends. See you tomorrow", Akhil replied. Jyotika nodded. "Bye guys", she said and was soon out of sight. "No wonder, time spent in beautiful company flies by so swiftly", Akhil said as the boys turned round and headed in the other direction.

"Where have you been guys? I was beginning to get a bit worried", Sahil said as soon as he saw them. "Don't worry, we were in good company", Akhil replied. "I hope you guys are not skipping the evening walk in the market. Remember, weekends are special, the sights are a real feast for the eyes", Sahil asked with a naughty smile. "I am sorry mate. I think I have had more than my share of excitement for the day. And am not sure if I can handle some more", Akhil replied.

"Hey Sameer bhaiya, what are you doing here all alone"? Rajeev asked. "Saxena ji has gone upstairs to have his dinner so I am just looking after the place in his absence. Why don't you come and join me, I could do with some company", he replied with a laugh. "Bhaiya, how long will you manage with such kind of company? I think you can do much better", Sahil said. "I don't know what you have in mind", Sahil said. "I see a lot of smart chicks taking a stroll in the evening. In fact, I see two of them outside just now. Why don't you give it a try", Sahil suggested almost pointing in the direction of the two girls outside. "Unlike you, I have my hormones under check. And moreover, I don't intend to become the target of public ire and get thrashed to pulp", Sameer replied.

"Bhaiya, what is the name of that girl in the red t-shirt? She looks cute, doesn't she"? Sahil asked. "Stop pointing your fingers, you idiot. She is Swati and lives in the building next to us", Sameer replied.

"Rajeev, how am I looking"? Akhil asked drawing an angry response. "I told you already, you look good as you always do. But if you keep the lady waiting she will definitely not like it", Rajeev replied. "Wish me luck then. Bye", Akhil said as he closed the door and made his way outside.

Jyotika was waiting for him just outside the institute building. She was dressed in an all-black ensemble and looked stunning.

"I hope I didn't keep this beautiful lady waiting for too long. Let's go to Bengali Sweets", Akhil said. "Tell me, is your friend really fasting today or is it just an excuse"? Jyotika asked. "Excuse for what"? Akhil asked. "Since he is not very outgoing, I thought it was just an excuse to avoid having lunch with me"? Jyotika replied. "Umm, nothing like that, I assure you", Akhil said in defence of his friend though he knew it did not sound too convincing. Jyotika went through the menu carefully before settling for the Bengali Special thali and lassi.

"On a serious note, what made you choose me to accompany you today? I mean, there are other girls in our class", Jyotika asked. "Well, I have never really thought much about that, you see. You are the first girl I started talking to. That is all I guess", Akhil replied with a confused look. "I am paying today. You don't get to be the good guy everyday", Jyotika said and grabbed the bill from Akhil's hand when he made a move to take out his wallet. "Shall I walk you back to the hostel"? Akhil asked when they were on the road. "No thanks, I can manage on my own", Jyotika said politely.

"In that case, I will leave you here. By the way, thanks for your company. That was fun. So can we meet again next Saturday"? Akhil asked. "No maybe some other time. I have only just arrived in Delhi and don't want to get too distracted", Jyotika replied. "Bye, see you on Monday", she said as she left.

"Welcome back, so is it the beginning of another love affair"? Rajeev asked with a smile. "No, on the contrary, she doesn't want to get distracted. That's what she told me when I asked her out next week", Akhil replied. "Well good for her. It clearly shows that not everyone in our class has come here to make friends and fall in love", Rajeev added with a laugh.

"So what do I do? Drown in agony or fall in love with those books and spend every waking hour leafing through them", Akhil said woefully. "Not necessarily. You can try and work your charm on that South Indian girl", Rajeev said. "You mean Tulika"? Akhil asked as his eyes lit up again. "See you already know those names by heart. She is not bad either", Rajeev said. "Stop pulling my leg, buddy", Akhil protested. "Okay, our exams are starting in a couple of month's time. How well prepared are you"? Rajeev asked.

"You know it well enough, dear. I don't even know the names of all the subjects properly", Akhil replied. "In that case, God can be your only savior. And please don't come to me with that scared-look a couple of days before the exams. I cannot be your savior every time", Rajeev said.

"Well, well. Seems like everybody is conspiring to turn their backs on me", Akhil said ruefully.

CHAPTER-15

"Rajeev, please fill my bucket also if you are going to the bathroom", Akhil said with his eyes barely open before going back to sleep. "Sure thing, but if you intend to go back to sleep again then please let me remind you that today is Sunday", Rajeev said. "It doesn't matter. We will request for home delivery. I will have my food right here in this room. Sundays are meant for rest and relaxation", he growled. "Fine, you lazy bum", Rajeev said.

"O my God! What was that"? Sahil said as he sat munching his chole bhatture. "I thought it was Akhil's tummy", Rajeev said. "No, I don't think so. I think that sound is coming from outside", Akhil said as he opened the door wide. "You are right. I think Dada Ji's in the toilet. I mean, he lets out those ear-splitting farts regularly every morning. By now I thought you guys were quite familiar with those sounds", Akhil said trying to suppress his laughter. "He wakes up early everyday and starts reciting those prayers loudly disrupting my sleep", he added.

"Where is Vinit? Haven't seen him around since the last couple of days", Sahil asked. "He has gone to his village in Rajasthan", Akhil replied. "Something seems to be troubling him of late", Rajeev said. "Have you seen the huge crowd queuing up outside to make phone-calls? Saxena Ji surely makes a lot of moolah on Sundays", Akhil remarked. "Good for him. He has a family to look after, remember", Rajeev said.

"Finally, another long and tiring day comes to an end", Akhil said as he got ready to leave the class room. "Hey guys! Please pay attention. We are organising a small get-together for you all this Sunday. Do check the notice board", said a guy from the senior batch.

"Do you have any questions"? He asked as he got ready to leave. Akhil raised his hand. "Bhaiya is there any dress code"? He asked. "Yes, all should come dressed in formals", the other guy replied. "Yippee, finally we get to have some fun. And for a change, someone else is going to pay for it, great", Akhil said. "Come let's go check the notice board", Sahil said. "This year our seniors have decided to club the management and computer science batches together to reduce expenses", Sahil said. "You know, Manish Pandey has been eyeing Sujata for some time now. I have a feeling something exciting is in store", Sahil said with a chuckle.

"Wait a second, who are these people? I don't remember hearing their names before", Rajeev said.

"Manish is the fellow who made the announcement and Sujata is the hottest chick in our class, you dumb-ass", Sahil replied.

"There goes the last", Akhil said as he carelessly flung a spiral bound heap of A-4 size pages aside. "Thank God, the ordeal is over", he continued even as he wiped off the beads of sweat forming on his forehead. "Have you checked your work thoroughly"? Rajeev asked.

"Yes, I have gone through every page thrice. I am not taking any chances at all. After all, if I screw up my assignments, I won't even stand a chance of making it to the next semester", Akhil replied.

"Now I can spend the next couple of days in getting ready for the party", he continued. "I see, instead of waiting why don't you get started right now", Rajeev said with a laugh. "You know, I have to ask Jyotika to give me company. It takes time as convincing her is not easy", Akhil said.

"What if she doesn't want to go to the party"? Rajeev

asked. “Now don't you dare make me angry again, Rajeev”, Akhil replied. “Come let's go. Professor Arvind is taking a tutorial class today and I don't want to be late”, Rajeev said as he led the way.

CHAPTER-16

"Stop ogling at her like that and concentrate on the accounting concepts instead", Rajeev whispered in Akhil's ears when he saw him looking frequently at Jyotika. "Why don't you just keep quiet and let me do what I like best? If you don't like it, you always have the option of looking the other way", Akhil replied.

"Hey Jyotika, can I speak to you for a second"? Akhil said as soon the professor and the students began making their way out of the class. "About what, Akhil"? Jyotika asked with a puzzled look. "It's regarding the fresher's party this Sunday. The three of us can go together. It will be fun", Akhil said desperately trying to impress her.

"Okay, but only under one condition", Jyotika said. "What"? Akhil asked. "I won't stay there beyond 6 pm", she replied. "As you wish, Madam", Akhil replied with a big smile. "Way to go brother! But who is the third person accompanying you", Rajeev asked.

"Who else but you", Akhil replied. "No way", Rajeev shook his head. "Now don't be a spoil-sport. Don't you see that girl agreed to go with us because she feels safe around you", Akhil said. "How can you be so sure"? Rajeev asked with a frown. "Just trust me on this, mate", Akhil said as he made his way out from the building with Rajeev following behind.

"Now stop fidgeting around and get dressed quickly", Akhil shouted at Rajeev. "Do I really have to"? Rajeev asked. "I don't remember having given you any other option", Akhil replied with a stern look. "Didn't I tell you that you too need to improve your confidence level and be a bit more outgoing", Akhil continued. By the time, they reached Jyotika's hostel, she was already waiting for them outside the gate. "Come let's go", Akhil said stepping aside to let the other two get inside the auto before him. "Any idea how far this place is from here"? Jyotika asked. "No. But what I have heard from some of my friends makes me believe it is going to be worth our time", Akhil replied.

"I think that is the place you guys are looking for", the auto driver, a soft-spoken fellow quite unlike the others the others they have encountered so far said as he got down and walked up to a watchman standing outside the gate of an imposing building. "Yes, this is it", he confirmed upon his return. "Thanks Uncle", Akhil said as he got out and paid the fare.

CHAPTER-17

Everything about the place they entered was fabulous starting from the massive wrought iron gate to the well-maintained lawns and ending of course with the imposing building itself that had sheer opulence stamped all over it.

"Let's sit over there", Jyotika said pointing towards the swimming pool. "Looks like most of the students have already arrived", Rajeev said. Just when they had found a place for themselves by the pool-side, someone began making an announcement.

"On behalf of all the seniors, I welcome you to this party. We will begin with a round of introductions which will be followed by light refreshments and some other activities. Dinner will be served at 9.00. Hope you all will enjoy this evening. Thank you".

All those who were standing nearby clapped briefly. "So our Pandey Ji is the thick of things once again", Rajeev said with a chuckle. "Excuse me guys", Akhil said and quickly made his way towards a corner where Sahil was standing with his friends. "I saw you guys but chose not to disturb you and your female companion", Sahil said with a hint of sarcasm. "Sorry, it's my fault. I should have informed you about our plan instead of slipping away quietly like we did. That is why I have come over to apologise the moment I saw you", Akhil said. "It's great to see you in such beautiful company. But at the same time, you shouldn't turn your back on your friends. Anyway, enjoy the evening", Sahil said patting Akhil on his back.

"I hate loud music and crowded places. In fact, this is the first time I am attending such a party", Jyotika said after taking a look round her. "Me too, it is only because of

Akhil that I am here. He left me with no choice", Rajeev replied. "Good to see you striking up a conversation finally with a beautiful young woman", Akhil said. "This outing is already showing some positive signs on you", he continued. "Stop pulling my leg and have your drink", Rajeev said pushing a glass in Akhil's direction. "Thanks a lot", Akhil said and gulped down the contents in no time. "Let's walk up to the other side of the pool. I think the introduction session is about to start", Rajeev said as he got up from his chair. "Yeah let's go", Akhil said.

"Okay juniors, please stand to one side. As soon as I sound the buzzer, I want you to step forward and introduce yourselves. The one whose performance is adjudged the best will win attractive prizes", announced a beautiful lady wearing a red dress.

CHAPTER-18

"She is Urvashi, a second year MBA student and winner of last year's Miss fresher contest. Beautiful, isn't she"? Akhil whispered in Rajeev's ear. "You said the same thing about Jyotika too, didn't you"? Rajeev asked. "Of course I did. But then there are other beautiful girls too", Akhil reasoned.

The students came and went until finally, it was the turn of a big fellow named Vishal with Jyotika bringing up the rear. "Hello everybody I am Vishal from Gurgaon", the burly fellow introduced himself. "Are you into sports or something? Your physique is impressive", Urvashi asked. "Yes Madam, I am a professional boxer", Vishal answered. "In that case, juggling two activities must be a tiring job for you. Isn't it"? Pandey said trying to pull his leg.

"I didn't get you", Vishal said looking confused. "How do you balance your studies and your boxing career"? Urvashi intervened trying to make things simple. "Oh! I don't have to box all the time. And I make adjustments as and when required", Vishal explained. Jyotika walked in next, to a big round of applause. And it was not surprising to see that most of those who were clapping were men much to Akhil's consternation. After all, beauty never ceases to attract.

"Hello seniors, I am Jyotika from Jammu. I enjoy listening to old Hindi songs and reading books", she began trying to keep things simple while Akhil listened intently. "That's too boring. A young girl like you listening to boring old songs and reading books all the time doesn't sound great. Can we have some music please? We want you to do a catwalk for us", Manish Pandey demanded.

Jyotika was taken aback at first but with unsure footsteps she began to walk up and down the makeshift stage to the tune of music but got into the groove towards the end which was met with loud applauding claps by almost everyone. “Thanks everyone for your co-operation. We will announce the results soon”. Urvashi announced and left quickly. “I just hope Jyotika wins the miss fresher crown this time. Nobody even came close to her today”, Akhil said getting excited.

“Let's see, there comes Manish Pandey with your new muse, Urvashi”, Rajeev said. “Let's not keep you guys waiting for too long. We have decide that the stars of this evening are Mister Rajeev and Miss Jyotika”, Urvashi announced.

“What the fuck! Did I hear it right?' Akhil muttered almost losing his balance and grabbing wildly at Rajeev's shoulder to avoid falling. You guys have done it. Oh! I am so happy”, Akhil shouted in joy even as he grabbed Rajeev in a tight hug. “Congratulations Rajeev”, Jyotika said as she came and stood near them. “Thanks and same to you”, Rajeev returned the compliment.

“I still can't believe that I have won this title. There were so many others who deserved it more than me”, Rajeev confessed. “Why do you say so? I don't know about the others but I think honesty and simplicity are you forte and the judges liked those two qualities in you”, Jyotika smiled. She looked so much more beautiful when she smiled. And this was the first time Rajeev silently observed and admired her beauty.

As the taxi screeched to halt outside Jyotika's hostel, Rajeev was suddenly jolted out from his thoughts. “It's time to start walking once again”, Akhil said as he gave Rajeev a slight push. “Okay guys, thanks for your company, good night”, Jyotika said as she closed the gate and walked into her hostel.

"How quickly good things come to an end, isn't it? Now let's take the long walk back to our room and have our dinner. I would have loved to stay till the very end", Akhil said. "How come you boys are back so early? Sahil called up some time ago and took permission from me to return at 11 pm saying that it was compulsory for all to stay on till the function ended. Is it true"? Saxena ji asked.

"Yes uncle, that's correct. But as I was not feeling well, we requested for permission to leave early", Akhil replied even before Rajeev could say anything. "What happened to you"? Saxena ji asked showing some concern. "Don't worry uncle, it's nothing serious. I am suffering from a mild fever since yesterday but already feeling a lot better now", Akhil said trying to reassure Saxena ji.

"Okay, you guys must be hungry. I will send Chandra downstairs with your food", Saxena ji said and got up to leave. "Thanks a lot for taking me to the party, dude. It's really the first time that I enjoyed being part of such an event", Rajeev said to Akhil after finishing his food. "I am glad that you enjoyed it. Now be prepared for some more fun. Your birthday is approaching and I have a surprise in store for you", Akhil said. "Okay, we shall see when the time comes. Let's go to sleep now", Rajeev said as he switched off the lights.

CHAPTER-19

"Well students, we now focus on Kuznets's characteristics of economic growth. As you all know he received the Nobel Prize in economics in 1971 for his pioneering work in the measurement and study of historical growth in national incomes in developing nations. The six characteristics are – high rates...... That boy sitting in the corner, what's his name", Professor Bujarbaruah roared in anger.

"Akhi... Akhil Sir", Rajeev replied with a stammer even as he pinched his friend to wake him up. Akhil, rudely jolted out of his slumber felt uneasy as all the eyes in the classroom were fixated on him. "Stand up and define death rate", the professor commanded him. "Sir, death rate is.........." Akhil hesitated. "What is dependency burden"? The professor continued in an unforgiving mood.

"I am sorry sir", Akhil replied with a downcast countenance. "So this is your level of concentration in the class. Don't come to my class if you are not interested. The others shouldn't suffer because of you", the professor said before leaving the class. "You should be a bit more attentive in the class. I cannot keep my eyes trained on you all the time", Rajeev said as they walked back after class. "Maybe I should have listened to you", Akhil answered ruefully.

"Good afternoon! Hope you guys have started preparing for the exams", Sameer asked. "I am starting serious preparation from tomorrow, bhaiya", Rajeev replied. "I am leaving for Luck now tonight to attend my sister's engagement ceremony. See you guys after a week", Sameer said as he left.

“If only you would have studied like this for a month things would have been a lot easier for you. But still it's great to see you study”, Rajeev said. “Do I have a choice”? Akhil replied in a voice that clearly highlighted how he hated studies. “Come on cheer up! You will have plenty of time for you other activities after a couple of weeks”, Rajeev said with a smile.

“Where is Sahil? I haven't seen him since yesterday evening”, Akhil asked. “He has gone to his uncle's place in Jamia Nagar and will return one day before the exams”, Rajeev replied. “Good for us, atleast we can have a few days of peace and quiet”, Akhil added.

CHAPTER-20

"Phew! What a relief", Akhil remarked as he emerged from the examination hall. "Don't be so happy because the results will be out in a week's time", Rajeev said. "Doesn't matter to me a lot because unlike you I just aim to secure pass marks", Akhil replied. "Now is the time for some fun. Let's wait for Sahil", he continued.

After a brief wait Sahil showed up along with a few of his class-mates. "Hey guys meet Arijit Das and Bidyut Bikash Bora. Both of them are from Assam", Sahil said as the others stepped forward and greeted each other. "I am organising a small party at my place. Why don't you guys join in? It will be fun", Arijit said. "Yeah sure, we would love to", Akhil replied. "Good. Sahil has my address. Be there by six so that you can leave by eight", Arijit said. "Okay", Rajeev nodded.

"Please stop next to that yellow building", Sahil said. "Are you sure this is the one we are looking for"? Rajeev asked. "Trust me on this mate. But if you are so unsure I will go upstairs and confirm that we have come to the right place", Sahil volunteered. "Fine, carry on", Rajeev said as he moved his legs to allow Sahil enough room to move out. Sahil hurried upstairs but came down soon after with a confused look on his face. "These buildings look so similar that you can't tell one from the other", he grumbled as he instructed the auto-driver to start his auto again. Suddenly Sahil's face lit up as he motioned to the driver to move in the direction of a shop. As the auto came to a halt, the boys saw Arijit come out of the shop carrying kitchen provisions.

"Hey, hope you guys had no problem in locating my place"? Arijit asked as he led the way into a building next to the shop. "Not at all", Sahil answered. "Have the other guys arrived already"? He continued trying to keep the conversation flowing in order to deny the opportunity to Akhil and Rajeev to embarrass him in front of Arijit. As the boys went in, they saw Bidyut Bikash Bora and another classmate of Sahil & Arijit busy playing cards while gorging on fried chicken legs, bhujia and other accompaniments and sipping something from a plastic glass every now and then. "Be at ease, guys", Arijit said. "By the way, he is Santonu from Nagaon. He is also in my class", he continued.

"So am I the only odd one out here"? Sahil asked with an expression that clearly showed he was feeling left out. "Arrey Sahil Bhai, you are the life of this party. We were eagerly waiting for a healthy dose of your naughty jokes to keep us happy", Arijit remarked trying to make him feel at home. "So shall we get started guys? I just remembered you two have to leave early", Arijit spoke again pointing at Rajeev and Akhil. "Count me in too. I don't want to spend the night roaming the streets", Sahil said sparking a burst of laughter from Bidyut and Santonu. "Must admit though, your hostel-owner is very strict. But the 9 pm deadline looks ridiculous", Bidyut mocked. "Okay guys, care to have some whiskey"? Arijit asked while pouring himself a drink. While Sahil moved forward and joined him, Akhil and Rajeev shook their heads. "Alright then, this is for you two", Arijit said as he handed Rajeev a bottle of coke.

"So how are studies progressing"? End semester exams are almost upon us", Santonu said. "That is his department. He will know best", Akhil said pointing towards Rajeev. "Very funny, isn't it Akhil? But you will be in big trouble if you don't pay some serious attention towards this department. Remember your mid-semester grades, do you"? Rajeev answered him. "Chill guys, exam is still some distance away", Bidyut spoke sensing some anger in Rajeev's voice. “I have ordered the food already, should be here soon”, Arijit said.

Just then, there was a knock on the door. “Must be the guy from Sethi's”, Arijit said as he got up and opened the door. As he walked back with the food packets and made his way to the kitchen, the tempting smell of tandoori chicken wafted into the living room making Bidyut and Sahil sniff the air noisily. “The tandoori chicken of this place called Sethi's is quite famous”, Arijit said while returning to join his friends. “Is it? I can't wait to have a go at it. Am feeling hungry already”, Sahil said making the others laugh. “Very well then, if you guys don't mind let the three of us finish our drink, while the two of you can start unpacking the food”, Arijit said pointing at Rajeev and Akhil. “Sure thing”, Rajeev said as he got up and followed Akhil into the kitchen. “Now let's get this thing done quickly. After dinner, we have to help in cleaning up the kitchen”, Rajeev said.

In a few minutes, the two boys had finished the task of serving the food and its appetizing smell ensured that nobody needed a second invitation when Rajeev yelled out that it was dinner time. “Umm delicious”, Bidyut exclaimed with his eyes closed as he dug into a chicken leg. “It surely is”, Akhil seconded him as he helped himself to some more fried rice. “Sahil bhai, how come you are so silent? Share one of your jokes with us atleast”, Santonu said. “When the food is so tasty I just love to close my eyes and enjoy the aroma of spices that have gone into it. But since you guys are insisting, let me share something with you. But let me tell you it's not a joke. Have you seen the tea-stall at the end of our lane”? Sahil asked looking in the direction of Santonu. “Do you mean the one close to our institute”? Santonu enquired. “Exactly, well I was on my way back from Kidwai Nagar last evening when I saw the daughter of the tea-stall owner in a corner of the park moving around nervously with Baldev, the gate-keeper of our institute. I am not sure, but from that distance it appeared to me as if he was trying to take advantage of the darkness and relative isolation by grabbing and squeezing her behind", Sahil said. "Are you sure"? Akhil asked, his eyes lighting up with excitement.

"Yeah, I am pretty sure about that. But I cannot say with certainty if the grabbing preceded the squeezing or vice-versa", Sahil said with a mischievous wink. "Tell me, why you are always the only person to spot such scenes"? Arijit asked trying to suppress his laughter. "I don't know buddy. It just happens that way. I guess I just end up at the right place at the right time", Sahil replied.

"See, even Baldev is having his share of fun. I feel you should express your feelings for Tulika openly as soon as you can or else you may lose the opportunity of romancing the lovely lady", Rajeev said looking at Akhil. "You know what I mean don't you? You should make your move before another competitor turns up," He added. "I will make my move at the right time but let me tell you, I have no such feelings for Tulika. Don't you know that I am interested in Jyotika"? Akhil said. "Oh, I am so sorry. But if the lady in question is Jyotika then I think the time to wait and plan your move is already up. I feel that there are too many guys who are vying for her attention already", Rajeev said.

"Let's see who ends up on the winning side. I am not losing my sleep thinking about my chances like you", Akhil responded. "I was joking Mr Lover boy. No need to get so worked up", Rajeev replied with a laugh. "Okay guys now let's help the host in cleaning up the place", Sahil said as he got up and proceeded towards the kitchen. "By the way, Rajeev is right, Akhil. If it's Jyotika whom you are interested in then you better make haste", Sahil said even as he continued washing the utensils.

“Thanks a ton for helping me clean up. Let's plan more such get-togethers whenever we feel like”, Arijit said after all the boys reassembled in the living room.”Sure, why not”, Akhil said. “Thanks for inviting us Arijit. I think we should get going now.” Rajeev said after checking the time on his watch. “You are always welcome”, Arijit said as he proceeded to open the door for his friends.

“These guys are having fun, aren't they? On the contrary, we have to rush back to hostel like kids just because of that stupid deadline”, Sahil said with a look of disgust on his face. Don't be so upset, such restrictions are required during student life. We are not here to party and have fun”, Rajeev said even as he instructed the auto-rickshaw driver on the route to take after crossing Bengali Sweets. “And I am sure five-six years later you will feel like thanking Saxena Ji over and over again. It is very easy to get distracted if there is too much freedom”, he added. You name him and there he is. Saxena Ji must be missing his most studious and sincere tenant today. Look how he is checking his watch anxiously”, Sahil whispered before opening the door and walking in. “I thought that you guys had forgotten about the timings tonight. Anyway, I hope you had your dinner because Aunty is not well today and Chandra is not that good a cook.” Saxena Ji said.

“Yes Uncle, we had our dinner at a friend's house. Don't worry”, Akhil replied.

CHAPTER-21

"Akhil hurry up, we are waiting for you", Rajeev yelled as soon as he finished drinking his glass of milk. "Still fifteen minutes left for classes to start. We will be there in plenty of time", Akhil said as he reached out for his glass of milk. "If you guys have finished arguing, can we proceed ahead"? Sahil asked with a frustrated look on his face. "Sure buddy, anything for you. And we were not arguing, by the way", Akhil said as he swung the door open for Rajeev and Sahil to pass. "How hot it is today. I just wish they would provide us a classroom in the second floor. It's so much better there", Akhil said. "Looks unlikely, Akhil. We will have to complete this semester before thinking about moving to a more spacious and well-ventilated classroom", Rajeev said. "I think you are right mate", Akhil replied. "Hurry up, I can already see Aman Sir walking towards our class", Rajeev said giving Akhil a nudge from behind.

"See you later, Sahil", Akhil shouted as he hurried along with Rajeev towards their classroom. "May I come in Sir", Rajeev asked gingerly as he knew that Professor Aman was not particularly fond of latecomers. "Try to be on time. Don't you remember what I told you guys last week", the professor said with a stern look on his face. "Sorry Sir, please excuse us this time", Rajeev said apologetically as he followed Akhil and took his seat. "We will reach in plenty of time, wasn't it what you said Akhil", Rajeev hissed under his breath. "I am sorry, mate. But I am a mere mortal and do commit mistakes every now and then", Akhil responded.

"Fine, now shut up and let me concentrate", Rajeev whispered even as he took out his book on Accounting Concepts and placed it on his desk. "Why is Jyotika absent today? Must be unwell, I guess", Akhil whispered in Rajeev's ear which drew nothing but an angry look from him. "Students, your end semester exams are just about a month away. We will revise whatever has been taught so far in the next few classes. So please go through the chapters and let me know if you have any doubts", the Professor said.

"Let me also remind you that three of your seniors failed last year and had to go all the way to Bilaspur to appear in the supplementary examination conducted by the University. So prepare well and don't take any subject lightly", he added just as he got ready to leave the class. "I don't know how I am going to deal with these two subjects", Akhil said. "Which two", Rajeev asked. "Accounting Concepts and Business Mathematics," Akhil replied back. "Formulate a strategy to deal with them or else just like Professor Aman said, be prepared for the journey to Bilaspur", Rajeev replied. "Hey guys, what's up", Arijit said when he saw Rajeev and Akhil standing outside their classroom. "I guess you missed your first class, right", Akhil asked. "Yes, I woke up late. Went to attend a party last night", Arijit replied. "No big deal. We still have two more classes to go before we can call it a day", Sahil said as he joined the others. "You are surely having fun Arijit. We are hopelessly stuck in that wretched place", Akhil said. "Why don't you guys shift to a rented apartment"? Arijit asked. "Santonu stays with three other guys in Amrit Nagar. He told me yesterday that they are planning to leave next month. You can speak to him if you are interested", Arijit continued.

"I have seen his place. It's not very far from here. And the location is not bad either", Sahil said. "Why don't you two let Sahil accompany you to Santonu's place today? Anyway, don't think I am forcing you. It's totally up to you guys." Arijit said. "It's okay mate. No harm in visiting a friend's place. We will visit him today evening itself", Akhil said after looking in Rajeev's direction.

"Good, as you wish. Even the owner of Santonu's apartment is cheerful and friendly unlike your landlord although he is much older than him." Arijit said trying to mimic Saxena Ji's expressions in such a funny manner that even Rajeev could not help laughing. "Okay then guys, see you later", Arijit said as he walked back to his classroom with Sahil.

CHAPTER-22

"I called up Santonu just now. He told me that he will be available anytime after five", Sahil said as he joined Akhil and Rajeev in the lobby. "Okay, let's check out his place then and find out if it's really as good as Arijit wanted us to believe", Akhil said.

"The locality is pretty decent", Sahil said as he led the way into a well-maintained building. "I think most of the residents of this building are Bengali", Rajeev said after having a quick look at the name plates attached to the doors at they went up the stair-case. "Not most, all of them are except Santonu and his flat-mates", Sahil said with a laugh. "There you are guys. This is where he stays", he continued even as he pressed the doorbell.

"Good evening guys. I was waiting for you", Santonu said as he opened the door and moved aside to let the three guys walk in. "I didn't see you in the college today. So I thought maybe you were unwell", Rajeev said. "No actually I went to Karol Bagh to purchase some scooter spare parts for my brother. My cousin is going home tomorrow so I went to his place in North Campus and gave him the things that I bought today", Santonu explained. "Great, you saved the courier charges", Sahil quipped. "Actually Arijit told us that your flatmates are going to leave soon", Akhil asked.

"Yes, they are leaving next month. One has completed his studies and is going home and the other two are planning to shift to North Campus to join some Civil Services coaching institute", Santonu explained. "So if you guys are interested, you can join me. I have already found one guy who is interested", he continued. "Can I see the rooms"? Akhil asked as he got up. "Sure, this way please", Santonu said as he led the way. "We have two bedrooms, two bathrooms, kitchen and the living room", Santonu said as he moved from one room to the other. "How much is the rent"? Rajeev asked. "You won't believe it. Only Rupees Six thousand per month", Santonu replied with an excited look on his face.

"You are really lucky. This place is much better than Arijit's and the rent is also very reasonable", Akhil said. "And the best thing is that the landlord is such a kind fellow. He doesn't mind if there is a delay in paying the rent and we even get invited occasionally for lunch", Santonu said. "I really like your place but can't make any commitment now about moving in next month. I need some time to think and discuss", Akhil said.

"Fine, take your time. You have a month to decide". Santonu said as he led Akhil back to the living room. "So what would you guys like to have, tea or coffee"? Santonu asked. "Let's have a cup of coffee each", Rajeev said as he followed Santonu into the kitchen. "May I know who the other guy is who is moving in with you? I mean, is he from our institute"? Akhil asked. "He is Kamaljeet, my classmate", Santonu replied. "You mean that short Punjabi guy from Guwahati. He is quite a character", Rajeev said with a laugh.

"Thanks for the coffee", Akhil said after washing the cup and placing it on the shelf. "Are you going to attend classes tomorrow"? He asked as he plonked down on the sofa with Santonu. "Yes, sure thing", Santonu replied.

"Thanks for giving us your time inspite of having such a hectic day", Rajeev said to Santonu as he came out of the kitchen with Sahil in tow. "No big deal guys. Hope to see you again soon", Santonu replied as he waved goodbye to the three.

CHAPTER-23

"Rajeev, Rajeev, wake up", Akhil shouted in excitement almost pulling his friend out of bed. "Rajeev opened his eyes and checked the time on his watch. "It is five 'o'clock now on a Sunday morning and I have never seen you wake up so early before. What's the cause of your excitement?" Rajeev asked with an angry look on his face. "Don't you know, today is the 21st of October, your birthday", Akhil replied.

"Well, it's just like any other day for me. You know I don't celebrate my birthday", Rajeev replied with a shrug of his shoulders after getting up from bed. "I know, but things are going to change a bit this time. We are going out today to celebrate your birthday", Akhil replied. "No I am not going out anywhere", Rajeev replied curtly. "Oh yes you are going out today", Akhil retorted. "In fact, we are planning to visit Appu Ghar today after lunch", he continued. "Great, but don't think I am going to fund your trip to the amusement park just because it happens to be my birthday today", Rajeev said. "Who said so? Everyone will contribute their share. Of course, you can arrange a special dinner for your hostel-mates if you feel like. Anyway, it's totally up to you", Akhil said. "Fine, we will discuss more after breakfast", Rajeev said as he proceeded to brush his teeth.

"Good morning & wish you a very happy birthday Rajeev", Vinit said when he saw Rajeev having his breakfast in the lobby. "Thank you, you went out somewhere"? Rajeev asked. "Yes, I went out to have my breakfast. Got fed up of the breakfast they are providing here. Can't they change the menu a bit", Vinit said. "By the way, the chole bhatture at Gupta's corner is delicious", he continued.

“Vinit, did you share your plan for the day with the birthday boy”? Akhil asked as he joined them. “Not yet, good that you reminded me”, Vinit said with a pat on Akhil's back. “I have invited a couple of my classmates to accompany us today. I am sure you won't mind, would you”? Vinit asked. “No, it's okay. So who all are going with us”? Rajeev asked. “Sameer bhaiya, Sahil, the three of us, Saxena Ji, his wife & son and two of my friends, that's it”, Vinit replied.

“Okay, at what time are we leaving”? Rajeev asked. “Hmm, 11.30 would be fine I guess”, Vinit replied after checking his watch. “Alright, let's get ready then. But don't you guys think with Saxena Ji and his wife for company, we won't be able to have fun at the park”? Akhil asked. “I know. But it was Saxena Ji who suggested the idea anyway. So asking him not to accompany us would be impolite. Don't you think”? Vinit countered. “Let them accompany us guys. We will still have a lot of fun, trust me”, Rajeev said as he stood up from his chair.

CHAPTER-24

"Come in", Rajeev yelled when he heard someone knock on his door. "Join me outside if you are not doing anything", Vinit said after opening the door. "Sure, why not", Rajeev said as he followed Vinit to the lobby.

"Rajeev, I want you to meet Shilpi & Neetu, my classmates. And ladies, since you were so eagerly waiting to meet the birthday boy, let me know what you think of him" Vinit said. "Happy birthday Rajeev", Shilpi said as she and her friend got up and shook hands with him. "And since you asked, I think he is quite good looking", she added looking in Vinit's direction which made Rajeev blush slightly. "Let me go upstairs and check if Saxena Ji is ready. Please excuse me guys", Rajeev said as he quickly made his way to the front door.

"Are you guys ready"? Saxena Ji asked as soon as he saw Rajeev standing near the front door. "Yes, we are Uncle. In fact, we are just waiting for you", Rajeev replied. "Okay then, give me five minutes. I will join you all downstairs", Saxena Ji replied. "Sure Uncle", Rajeev replied as he headed back to join his friends.

"So how long will it take him to join us"? Vinit asked looking impatiently at his watch. "Not more than a few minutes", Rajeev replied. "There he is", Vinit said heaving a sigh of relief. "Come let's go. Sahil & Sameer Bhaiya are already waiting outside for us", Rajeev said as he led the way. "Let's hire three autos from here. Heard a lot about the place, although this will be my first visit", Saxena Ji said as he got inside an auto with his wife and son.

"Why are you with us Rajeev? You should have given company to Shilpi. As it is, she finds you quite good-looking, isn't it"? Sahil said with a naughty smile. "Don't worry, Vinit is there to give her company," Rajeev replied. "That's true. But my dear friend, don't you think you are letting go of a good opportunity to spend a fun-filled, romantic evening. That lady is interested in you, moreover, by giving her company you could have allowed the three of us the luxury of travelling in some comfort", Sahil replied.

"So you want me to flirt with that lady just because you wanted some more leg-room. How mean of you! I have heard that people are ready to even sacrifice their lives for the sake of friendship. And you can't even tolerate some minor discomfort for your friend", Rajeev said trying to make fun of Sahil. "Please don't be under the illusion that I am going to sacrifice my life for anyone. My life is precious." Sahil retorted making everyone laugh.

CHAPTER-25

"Looks like, we have reached our destination finally. Time to disembark", Sameer said as he moved towards the gate where Saxena Ji was waiting. "We want the birthday special tickets. I believe a special scheme is on these days", Saxena Ji spoke to the man inside the ticket counter. "Yes Sir. But before that we would like to know who in your group is celebrating his birthday today. And we would also like to see some kind of proof so that we can be sure of his birth-date", the man replied.

"Sure thing", Rajeev said as he moved forward and produced a copy of his birth certificate at the counter. A few minutes later Rajeev joined the others with the entry tickets, fancy wrist-bands, unlimited ride and ice-cream coupons & a surprise birthday gift.

"Come let's go inside", Rajeev said to everyone after handing them their entry tickets. "Let's go for a boat-ride first and then we will head towards the bump-cars", Akhil said almost pulling Rajeev along in excitement.

Shilpi, Akhil, Rajeev and Vinit got into one boat while the others in the group chose to watch from a distance. "Damn it, this boat is full of mosquitoes and the water smells awful. Looks like they have not cleaned this pond for quite some time", Rajeev said. "Hmm, you are correct. Let's start pedalling. I too do not want to spend too much time on this boat", Vinit said. "Sure thing, let's keep this boat ride as short as possible. Don't want to tire myself out pedalling this boat. Even the pedals are so slippery", Rajeev replied throwing his hands up in disgust.

"Let's head in that direction. The bump-car ride will be a welcome change after our not so pleasant boat-ride",

Akhil said. “Hey, this is really cool”, Akhil shouted at Rajeev even as he manoeuvred his car past Vinit's. “It really is fun”, Rajeev nodded looking in Akhil's direction. Just then, Rajeev's car rammed into Shilpi's, making her let out a mild shriek. The ride continued for five minutes & Rajeev's car thudded into her thrice. On the last occasion, the lady was almost thrown off her car. This prompted a visibly embarrassed Rajeev to apologise to her repeatedly the moment the ride was over.

“Either you or your car seemed to have developed a liking for that lady. I can't believe that collided with her car thrice in five minutes. And on the last occasion, you almost threw her out by crashing sideways. I just hope that your intentions are noble and you have no plans to hurt the young lady”. Vinit said to Rajeev with a mischievous smile as they started walking towards the giant wheel. “That is not the case with me. I can assure you of that. However, I can't say with certainty about that car that I drove. And by the way, I have no such intentions”, Rajeev replied.

“This looks a bit scary”, Sahil said. “You can give it a miss, if you want to”, Rajeev said. “No way, I am not going to reduce myself to laughing stock especially in front of the two ladies whom we have for company”, Sahil replied. “Very well then, do what you feel like”, Akhil advised.

“Hey Rajeev, can I join you on this ride? I don't think I will be able to make it alone”, Shilpi asked, her eyes fixed on the empty seat next to Rajeev. “Sure you can”, he replied moving aside to allow her some more space to sit. “Alright, strap on your respective seat belts. The ride will start in a couple of minutes”, a hoarse voice called out from below. Seeing Shilpi fiddle with her seat belt in an unsure manner, Rajeev motioned to her how to fasten it. “Thanks. The longer one waits for the ride to start the more nervous one feels, isn't it”? She asked. “Well, you are correct”, he replied even as he caught Akhil winking at him through the corner of his eye but choose to ignore him completely.

As the motor of the giant wheel sprang to life and picked up speed, Shilpi grabbed Rajeev's arm and held on tightly. “It's okay, don't be scared. It will be over soon”, Rajeev uttered feeling uneasy. As the wheel gained more speed, she started moving closer & closer to him till her body touched his. Rajeev could feel the softness of her body and the shape of her twin assets as her body brushed against him giving him goose-bumps. “I am feeling scared. Please tell them to stop the ride”, Shilpi said even as she grabbed Rajeev's left arm and pressed it tightly against her bosom making him shift uncomfortably in his seat. He tried desperately to ignore the sensation caused by the softness of her nipples pressing tightly against him but the effects were beginning to show and his manhood rose slowly until the bulge in his trousers became impossible to ignore.

He tried sitting cross-legged in his seat in order to hide his erection from Shilpi's view but only ended up drawing her attention towards him. “What happened? You look as if you are in some kind of discomfort”, she asked with a look of concern on her face without loosening her grip on his arm. “No..... no, it's okay. I am alright”, Rajeev mumbled even as he pressed his legs together tightly just to make sure that Shilpi did not get a peek-a-boo of his manhood which was making tents out of his trousers. She thrust a long confused glance at him but not knowing what was wrong with him decided to keep quiet.

Finally, the ride was over and it was time to get down. While Shilpi & the others got down quickly making way for a group of enthusiastic young children who were eagerly waiting for their turn, Rajeev stayed put in order to let his erection subside. “Hello bhaiya, don't you want to come down? Please make way for the kids here”, the ride operator called out. “Sorry, just felt a bit dizzy after the ride, that is why I decided to relax for a few minutes”, Rajeev said even as he adjusted his underwear slightly to make sure his prick was in its proper place before getting up.

“You can take another ride if you want to since you have got those special tickets but not immediately after the first ride. Other people will object, you see”, the operator said, this time sounding a bit more polite. “One ride is more than enough”, Rajeev said and thanked the man as he passed by. “Now let's head for the main attraction of the park, the roller-coaster”, Akhil said enthusiastically.

“This one looks a bit scary. It hurtles down at a great speed from that height. I think I am going to skip this one”, Mrs Saxena said pointing to the spot from where the coaster begins its downward descent at a great speed. “Don't worry. Nothing will happen to you”, Saxena Ji said as he held his wife's hand and made her take a seat next to him. The slow journey to the top was uneventful. But the moment it made its downward descent, everyone began screaming wildly while trying to grab on to anything they could lay their hands on till the moment the ride came to an end after splashing through a pool of water.“So that brings our day of fun and celebration to an end. Let's head back before it's too late”, Saxena Ji said perhaps sensing that the boys were planning to prolong their celebration for some more time. “Yes uncle, let's go”, Sameer said.

“I am not letting you off so easily, Rajeev”, Shilpi said breaking the long reign of silence on the way back. “Why so”? Rajeev replied. “I was hoping that you would take us out for dinner”, Shilpi replied. “I am so sorry. But I think you already know the rules of our hostel, don't you", Rajeev said. "I do. Since I am excusing you today, promise me, that you will take me out for lunch next week", Shilpi came closer & whispered in Rajeev's ear. "Err.... sure. Any day you want. Just let me know when you are free", Rajeev said with an unconvincing smile. "Please stop at the next intersection", she told the auto-driver who nodded his head. "I have to purchase some vegetables so I will get down here", she explained to Rajeev and Vinit.

"Okay, as you wish. See you tomorrow. We have a class at 9 in the morning", Vinit said. "Sure", she replied.

"You are one lucky guy. Shilpi is also beginning to show a lot of interest in you", Akhil said while taking a leisurely stroll after dinner in the corridor outside his room. "Can't a guy & a girl just be friends?" Rajeev said throwing his hands wide in protest. "Yes, that is possible. But when a girl presses her body against you so tightly on the slightest pretext, you can be sure she has something more than friendship in mind", Akhil added with a wink. "I don't think so", Rajeev replied. "Well, we will find out soon", Akhil retorted.

CHAPTER-26

Rajeev's mobile beeped while he was on his way back from his institute, it was a text message from Shilpi. "Good morning! Where are you"? She wrote. "Good morning! How are you doing"? Rajeev messaged her back. "What are you doing in the afternoon tomorrow"? She asked. "Not much. I spend the weekends in the hostel mostly. May go out for a walk in the evening", he wrote. "Then join me for lunch tomorrow. My room-mate is going out early & will return late in the evening. And I hate to spend the day all alone on a holiday", she replied.

"And by the way, don't think that I am going to cook for you. We will order the food from somewhere. Your birthday treat is still due, remember", she added quickly. "Okay, as you wish", Rajeev replied. "Okay bye. See you at 11 am tomorrow near the Mother Diary outlet. Please be on time and don't keep me waiting", she concluded.

"Akhil, I am going to INA market. Do you need anything"? Rajeev asked. "No thanks. But why do you need to walk all the way to that market when you can easily buy what you need from Kotla"? Akhil asked. "Are you really going to the market or do you have some other plans up your sleeve"? He added with a frown. "No other plans, I assure you. Have your lunch on time and don't wait for me", Rajeev said patting his friend on his back as he went out.

"Hi, thanks for coming", Shilpi said & smiled at him the moment Rajeev reached the designated meeting point. "Would you like to have an ice-cream"? Rajeev asked. "Sure. Vanilla flavour for me", she replied. "Okay Miss," Rajeev said as he handed her an ice-cream cup. "Thank you", she smiled. "You are welcome", Rajeev replied. "How far do you stay from here?" he asked her as they moved towards the Kotla Mubarakpur market. “Well, not very far. Do you see that big electronics showroom on your right”? She asked. “Yes, I do”, he replied. “I stay just behind that shop”, she said.

“Your place is quite spacious even though it is a bit noisy outside and the lane somewhat congested”, Rajeev said after entering the single bedroom apartment. “Yeah, I know. But it is not easy to find a good & secure place to stay for girls everywhere in Delhi. Our landlady is really kind and helpful and I love this place”, she replied. “Good for you. I am sorry if I offended you in any manner by what I said just now”, Rajeev said apologetically. “It's alright. You needn't feel sorry”, she replied. “Who is your room-mate? Is she too from Assam”? Rajeev asked. “No, she is from Patna and her name is Trupti. She is my class-mate”, Shilpi replied.

“So what would you like to have tea or coffee”? She asked. “It's okay. I am not hungry. Instead, let's decide what we are going to eat”, Rajeev replied. “I insist. Tell me, tea or coffee”, she asked again. “Okay, in that case a cup of coffee would suit me fine”, he replied.

“That's more like it. Since today is your first visit, I must appear courteous and make you feel at home”, she replied with a laugh. “Please have a seat. I will join you in five minutes”, she added. “Sure”, Rajeev replied, plonked down on the sofa & picked up the newspaper lying on the table. “There you go”, Shilpi said on her return and placed two cups of coffee on the table accompanied by some biscuits and cupcakes. “Thanks”, Rajeev said and picked up his cup.

“So what do you want to have for lunch”? Rajeev asked. “Let's order two special thali from Bengali Sweets, chilli chicken, drums of heaven and fried rice from Magic Forest and two cold coffee with ice-cream from Kent's”, she said. “Phew! That's a pretty long list”, Rajeev exclaimed. “It has to be. After all, we don't celebrate birthdays everyday”, Shilpi reasoned. “Hmm, I agree with you on this one. Let's start making the calls right away”, Rajeev said as he took out his mobile from his trouser pocket.

CHAPTER-27

"Thanks for the treat. That was the best lunch I have had since I came to Delhi", Shilpi said while settling down on her bed after finishing her chores in the kitchen post lunch. "You are welcome. And by the way, you forgot to thank me for helping you wash the dishes after lunch", Rajeev replied with a smile. "Well, I told you I can manage on my own but it was you who insisted, so I am not going to thank you for that", she replied. "Oh yeah, that's very clever of you", he said.

"So what do you do apart from your studies"? She asked. "Not much. I mostly go out with Akhil for a walk in the evenings. And when I am alone, I prefer to go and sit quietly at the park in Kidwai Nagar & observe the giant mausoleum glowing in the bright white light from a distance", he replied. "Such a boring life you have had so far. Never been to a disco or a party at a friend's place"? She asked.

"Have never been to a disco thus far and I went to a friend's place for a party just once. In fact, the outing with you guys was my first group outing in Delhi", Rajeev admitted. "Do you have a girl-friend"? She asked even as she inched closer to him slightly. "Not yet", he replied. "Any plans on getting one in the near future"? She asked. "No, I don't think so. Why did you ask"? He replied with a confused look. "Just felt like asking, dude. Don't look so worried", she replied. "No, I am not", he said.

"Good for you. Just relax and let things take its own course", she replied with a mischievous wink even as she started running a finger through his hair. "Close your eyes & lean back", she said although the way she pushed him back slowly yet firmly made it difficult to make out whether it was a request or a command. Rajeev could feel the soft skin of her hands brush against his face as she leaned forward and the sensation caused by her warm breath blowing against his neck made him feel something which he had never felt before.

"I don't think we should be doing this", Rajeev said hesitatingly. "I see. And what if I won't stop doing it?" Shilpi said biting her lips provocatively & resting her breasts lightly on his chest. "I can feel you there. Getting a nice hard-on, aren't you"? She said while poking his manhood repeatedly with her right knee.

Rajeev just lay still, not knowing what to do. His mind wanted him to push her away and run but his body wanted him to squeeze her tightly in his arms and explore every inch of her soft but well-formed body. She moved closer and planted a long, passionate kiss on Rajeev's lips while she started moving her arms up & down slowly over his chest. Rajeev closed his eyes & felt the softness of her lips press against his. He was not sure what he was supposed to do for he had never indulged in such acts of passion before.

"Just relax & enjoy. I am going to make you feel real good", she said and slid her hands underneath Rajeev's vest and began running her hands up & down on his chest once again. She continued in this way for some time slowly increasing the intensity as she progressed. "O my lord! What do you have there"? She asked & pointed a finger at Rajeev's crotch. "You surely are game for some more fun, aren't you"? She added with a wink and proceeded to unzip Rajeev's trousers which she pulled down to his thighs within no time.

Rajeev tried not to look down because he could feel his dick throbbing wildly. Shilpi started rubbing her palms on his thighs this time while her gaze remained fixed on his manhood which had already reached alarming proportions owing to the attention being showered by her. She paused briefly, and then lowered her lips slowly over his prick while she held on to his thighs to support her weight.

She began circling her tongue all over and then ran her fingers slowly along the length of his prick. “Hmm, I can see you are all hard & raring to go.

Rajeev began moaning in pleasure and ecstasy. His hands slowly reached out in Shilpi's direction to push her face towards his manhood. As if sensing what he wanted, she quickly pulled his trousers all the way down and watched in amazement as his massive dick swung from side-to-side. Slowly, she moved forward, her lips shaking in anticipation as they neared his thighs. She reached out with her hands, grabbed his love tool with both her trembling hands & wrapped her lips around it, slowly, as if silently admiring it's girth, taking as much of it as she possibly could.

When she knew she could take no more, she took a deep breath and began running her tongue up and down his impressive length while making sure to establish eye contact with him every now and then. She traced a couple of her fingers to the top to wipe off the few drops of love juice, the stickiness and warmth of which made her even more excited. She got up, made Rajeev follow her while she bent down slightly holding on to a chair for support.

CHAPTER-28

After some persuasion, she managed to make him enter her from behind. Though fully aroused & excited, Rajeev was unsure and looked clumsy in the beginning but owing to words of constant encouragement from her, he finally managed to get his act together.

After some time, she motioned Rajeev to stop. She led him to her bed where she laid on her back, spread her legs apart and made him push his manhood inside her. He began slowly but increased the pace of his thrusts when he figured out what he was supposed to do.

Shilpi winced in pain every now and then but she did not complain because she knew that Rajeev was no more in a mood to let go. She wrapped her legs round his behind while she bit her lower lip to muffle her screams. She grabbed on to his left arm for support when he started pounding harder with every stroke going deeper and deeper into her and spreading her in the process.

She wanted to be in control again after some time so she brought he legs together, pushed Rajeev away slightly and got up on her feet. “Come here and lie down”, she commanded, almost dragging him to bed. She made him lie down on his back, gave a few tugs to his prick with her left hand and straddled him, holding on to his shoulders for support as she lowered her behind slowly, pushing him into her inch by inch.

She began slowly, moving her behind in a slow circular rhythmic motion before increasing her pace as she began bobbing up and down on his love tool. She could feel his body tighten as he grabbed her waist tightly before letting loose his hot, sticky warmth inside her. She on her part just closed her eyes and felt his warmth flood her inside. Tired and drained after their passionate union, they collapsed into each other's arms & fell asleep...

Rajeev was the first to wake up. He checked his watch first and then his mobile. “Gosh!” he exclaimed. “I must leave now. There are seven miss call notifications from Akhil's number,” he said and got up to go to the bathroom for a quick shower when Shilpi opened her eyes and grabbed his arm. “Where are you going”? She asked. “It's already 4 o' clock. I think, I should leave now,” he answered. “Why are you in such a hurry to leave? You still have a good five hours to go before that 9 pm deadline,” she reasoned. “Hmm, but I told Akhil ....,” Rajeev began but was stopped by Shilpi who got up & placed her hand over his mouth. “Your friend will do fine without your presence for a few hours so please don't make such a silly excuse”, she said after removing her hand from his mouth & planting a kiss on his lips. She followed it up with another kiss and traced a finger through his hair. She moved closer, held him in a tight embrace for some time & then slid down slowly running her hands over his chest and thighs almost burying her pink painted finger nails into his flesh as she went downtown on him once again.

Rajeev did not hesitate this time. He couldn't, because very soon he set about on his task to explore every inch of her body with his hands and tongue. After the initial exploration, their bodies entwined together culminating in an explosive union satiating their carnal desires.

After resting for some time, both went for a shower. “Thanks a lot for everything. The food was tasty but what followed next was even better”, Shilpi said with a wink while she watched Rajeev get dressed. “You are most welcome. Though I can't say what we did was morally correct, nevertheless, I surely enjoyed it”, he replied.

“You know, sometimes one should just let go of all

inhibitions and enjoy life. All these issues relating to right or wrong don't bother me. My motto in life is simple, life is short and uncertain so enjoy it while you can," she replied.

"Hmm, quite a statement, I must admit. Even then, I feel some caution is advisable", Rajeev replied as he got up and walked to the door.

"Bye", Shilpi waved at him as he went down the stairs. Rajeev waved back and went on his way.

CHAPTER-29

“Looks like you had more than just a leisurely stroll at the market, didn't you”? Akhil questioned Rajeev the moment he entered his room. “Well, I met Shilpi on the way and she insisted on having lunch together. And I had to oblige”, Rajeev replied.

“I see. So you had a great outing day today. I am sure you were too busy to even answer your phone, weren't you”? Akhil asked angrily. “I am extremely sorry. It won't happen again, I promise”, Rajeev replied. “You better be. By the way, there is something about this whole thing that I don't find convincing”, Akhil said with a confused look.

“I already apologised to you, didn't I. So let's stop discussing about it any further”, Rajeev said trying to steer clear of explaining the events that took place during the day. “Let's start preparing for the end semester exams from tomorrow. We have only two week's time left”, Rajeev said trying to change the topic of discussion.

**

“Just thinking about the exams gives me nightmares. I don't know how I am going to pass my financial accounting & Business mathematics papers”, Akhil said. “Don't worry. We will sit together tomorrow and study these two subjects first”, Rajeev replied trying to look cheerful even though he too was unsure about his friend's chances of scoring pass marks in those two subjects.

“Exams will be over soon but we haven't decided about shifting to Amrit Nagar. We have to let Santonu know about our decision soon. Can't keep him waiting for too long”, Akhil said. “We will discuss that after the exams. And I do feel that it would be better for us if we remain here”, Rajeev replied.

“In that case, you are free to stay in this wretched hostel. I have decided to move in with Santonu as soon as our exams are over”, Akhil replied. “Don't be in such a hurry to leave the place. I have a feeling that you will regret this decision”, Rajeev said. “We will see about that. How do you know that without giving it a try? “As far as I am concerned, the matter is closed for discussion. You decide and act according to what you feel would be best for you”, Akhil replied and left the room. Rajeev got up & followed his friend outside. “Look, I am more bothered about what is good for us. So if we have to move out from here, we will do it together”, he said and walked away.

CHAPTER-30

Saxena Ji was sitting in the lobby with a cup of tea when Rajeev walked up and sat opposite to him on the sofa. "Is everything okay, Rajeev? You look a bit worried to me", Saxena Ji asked. "Uncle we are planning to vacate the hostel next month", Rajeev replied. "What? I mean have you informed your parents. They are definitely not going to be happy with the decision that you have made," Saxena Ji replied. "My parents have already granted me their permission", Rajeev replied. "Okay then. As you wish. As per the rules, you have to vacate your hostel positively on the last day of next month. And your security deposit will be adjusted against next month's rent. It's your life, so you decide what is best for you. But remember son, you are here to study and to make a career not for fun and enjoyment", Saxena Ji said tersely & left in a hurry.

Rajeev got up and stood near the door. He looked at the bright lights illuminating the lane. He was not sure whether he had made the right decision but hoped that it would not have a negative impact on his life.

"Come and sit with me for a minute", Saxena Ji motioned to Rajeev when he saw that the two boys had almost finished loading their belongings onto the minivan. "I don't know what prompted you to leave this place but I know that you are different from the other guys you are moving out with. So if you ever feel that you made a mistake by leaving this hostel and want to return, I would be happy to welcome you back", he continued.

"Thanks a lot Uncle. I shall keep that in mind. I can never thank you enough for all the support and guidance that you have given me", Rajeev replied and touched Saxena Ji's feet as he moved out to the street.

"Rajeev, you can keep your belongings in my room for the time being. We will arrange everything tomorrow", Santonu said as he helped Akhil and Rajeev in unloading their belongings from the van. "Phew! There goes the last one", Akhil said as he placed a bucket on the floor & proceeded to pay the driver. "Feeling relieved finally. There is no Saxena uncle to nag me at every step", Akhil said as he collapsed on the sofa.

"Have you guys decided which room you want to occupy"? Santonu asked as he handed everyone a glass each of chilled water. "Thanks, I will stay in this room. It is large and airy. You can take the other room if you don't mind", Akhil said pointing at Rajeev.

"Since you guys have just moved in & are feeling tired, I have done the cooking tonight. From tomorrow, we will share the work", Santonu said. "Sure buddy, by the way, where is the other guy you were talking about"? Rajeev asked. "He has gone to his local guardian's house in North Campus. I think he will be back tomorrow." Santonu replied.

"I have cooked dal, subji and rice. No fancy stuff. If you want something extra you can order from A1 dhaba nearby or any other place that you prefer." he continued. "Yes, let's order Chicken Afghani from Sethi's. After all, we must celebrate the occasion, isn't it"? Akhil said as he got up to make the call.

"We will organise a small party this coming Sunday and maybe invite a couple of our friends, if it's okay with you guys", he continued. "Sure, why not. We can invite Arijit, Sahil and Sameer as well", Santonu nodded in approval. "I don't know about Sameer but the other guys will surely turn up", Akhil replied.

"How is everything? Hope you like the subji", Santonu asked. "Yes, it is delicious. Please pass me the bowl", Rajeev said as he helped himself to some more of it. "Even the chicken is delicious. I think we can order from Sethi's for our party on Sunday", Santonu said as he looked around for approval. "Sure we can", Akhil nodded in consent.

CHAPTER-31

"Hey guys wake up. The landlord is waiting outside and he wants to have a chat with you all", Santonu said almost pulling out Akhil from his bed. "Can't we have the discussion sometime later", Akhil grumbled. "I surely can't say that to the owner. Come on, he won't talk to you for an eternity. And besides it is already 7 am. Don't you want to go to college"? Santonu continued.

"Okay fine, give me two minutes", Akhil said and hurried into the bathroom. "Hello uncle", Akhil said as he greeted the landlord after Santonu introduced him to a sixty something, fairly tall & well-dressed gentleman. "Hi, I am B.B. Mozumdar. Santonu must have told you about me as well as about the rent and the rules and regulations", the landlord asked. "Yes uncle", both Akhil & Rajeev nodded in unison.

"Okay then. There is not much for me to add in that case. You can come & go as you please. Just make sure there is no unnecessary commotion. If you have an occasional get together, just ensure that the other residents don't feel disturbed. I would also be happy if you have fewer female guests. That's all", Mr Mozumdar said as he got up to leave. "I wish you guys a pleasant stay", he said as he closed the door and left the room.

"Your owner surely is a very friendly person. I am beginning to love this place already", Akhil said with a smile. "We will see about that. Now let's have our breakfast & get ready for college", Rajeev said as he went into the kitchen to help prepare breakfast.

That day while returning from class, Akhil invited his friends over for the party. "Okay guys. See you on Sunday", Santonu reminded Sahil and Arijit as he left his college campus.

CHAPTER-32

"So I hope Akhil is having no problem at all in settling down. He was so eager to leave the hostel. It appeared to me as if he would have dragged Rajeev along with his luggage had he not willingly accompanied you here", Arijit joked after taking a sip of coffee. "I would have surely. But all that is now behind us so let's celebrate", Akhil replied. "Guys tell me what do you want to have for dinner?" Rajeev asked. "Biriyani for me", Arijit added. "Order Tandoori chicken for me", Sahil joined in. "Okay so menu is decided. Biriyani, Tandoori chicken, dal makhni, navratan korma, rasmalai & salad prepared in our own kitchen. Does anybody have any objections"? Akhil asked.

"None at all, Sir", the other replied in unison. While Rajeev placed the order, the others settled down for a game of cards. "Well guys, as you can see luck is not on my side today. Let's have some music, shall we"? Arijit said after getting rid of the last card in his hand. "Sure, why not", Santonu replied as he played a soft romantic number by Zubeen.

"I feel so relaxed every time I listen to an Assamese song. Makes me feel as if I am at home with my family", Arijit said leaning back on his chair with his eyes closed. "Don't get so emotional now. I don't want you to spoil the mood of the other guys here", Akhil replied with a wink.

"I won't do that buddy, don't worry. Just felt like sharing my thoughts with you guys. Even with good friends like you for company, I still miss my home occasionally", Arijit replied. Just then, the door bell rang. "We will talk about our homes later. Now tell me who all are feeling hungry", Rajeev said as he got up to pay the delivery boy.

“We all are feeling hungry”, they erupted in a chorus even before Rajeev could place the packets on the kitchen counter. “Very well then, come and help me serve the food while I get the salad ready”, Rajeev replied & hurried into the kitchen.

“Umm, this Biriyani is simply amazing. And I really like the salad. Pass me some more please”, Arijit said as he helped himself to some more salad and Biriyani. For some time, nobody spoke a word as each one concentrated on relishing the food on their plates.

CHAPTER-33

"Well guys, now follow me to the kitchen & help me in cleaning up", Akhil said with a burp. "Thanks for everything guys. I think such get-togethers should be a monthly affair from now on", Arijit said as he plonked down on the sofa with a contented expression on his face.

"Count us in", Akhil & Santonu shouted out in unison. "Not a bad idea at all. Even I am interested", Rajeev said after some thought. "Let's have the next one at my place", Arijit volunteered. "Okay guys. I have to leave now", Sahil said as he got up from the sofa. "I will drop you at your hostel. Let's go", Arijit said. "Thanks. That would be a great help. Don't feel like walking all the way to the hostel after such a heavy meal", Sahil said as he proceeded towards the door. The rest of the boys accompanied them downstairs. "Okay guys, see you tomorrow ", Arijit said as he rode away on his bike.

"We had a great evening. I am going to bed early tonight. Don't want to miss the 8 am class as we have a test tomorrow", Santonu said after closing the door. "Okay guys, see you in the morning. Good-night", Rajeev said and proceeded towards his study table. Akhil sat down on the sofa & turned on the TV. "Don't you want to sit for the test tomorrow"? Rajeev asked. "I am not going to attend the first class tomorrow. I will join you after 10 am", Akhil replied.

"What about the test"? Rajeev asked with a frown. "I am not prepared for the test. Moreover, the marks secured in the test won't be considered while determining our final grades", Akhil reasoned. "But that does not mean you should take it lightly", Rajeev countered.

"Now come on Rajeev. Don't you start lecturing me

about what is right or wrong. Why don't you go & study"? Akhil replied rather rudely. Rajeev stared at Akhil for a moment and walked away shaking his head.

Akhil tuned in on the music channel turned up the volume slightly and plonked down on the sofa.

CHAPTER-34

"Good- morning and all the best for the test", Sahil said when he saw Rajeev and Santonu near the college gate. "Where is Akhil? Why does he not attend classes regularly"?Sahil asked.

"He is a very lazy guy. Thinks he is in Delhi for everything other than studies. I just hope he mends his ways soon. I want to be the last person to see him suffer", Rajeev said. "Don't worry. Everything will be alright", Santonu said. "Okay, we will meet after class. Bye for now", Sahil said & entered his classroom.

"I am feeling very hungry. Let's head to Gupta Ji's tea stall", Rajeev said after finishing his test. "Yeah sure", Sahil said and walked together with Rajeev towards the main road. "I don't see Akhil anywhere. Maybe, he is still sleeping. I don't think he is going to attend classes in the second half as well", Sahil continued. "I hope not. After all, his attendance figures are very poor & I doubt if he would be allowed to sit for the exams", Rajeev answered. "Well, let's head back to class. And since you are Akhil's closest friend, I guess you are the only sane voice he will listen to", Santonu said pointing at Rajeev.

"Akhil, I want to discuss something with you. Please come and sit with me" Rajeev said the moment he reached his room. "Yes, what is it"? Akhil answered with an irritated look. "When are you going to take your studies seriously? I mean, earlier you attended the classes regularly but now you have stopped doing that also", Rajeev asked. "Who gave you the right to talk to me in this manner"? Akhil thundered as he stood up all of a sudden & pointed a finger in Rajeev's direction. "Cool down, I am just asking you", Rajeev replied. "Don't you start behaving as if you own me, I am not answerable to you", Akhil said and left the room in a jiffy after closing the door with a huge thud.

CHAPTER-35

"Hello Rajeev, are you unwell today"? Jyotika asked jolting him out of his thoughts. "No, I am okay. What made you think so"? He asked. "I have been observing you since last week. You appear lost in some thoughts. You can share any issue you are facing if it isn't too personal", she replied. "It's nothing personal Jyotika. I am worried about Akhil, that's all", Rajeev replied. "Let's go upstairs. The cool breeze will make you feel better", she said, leading the way.

"Akhil is a mature guy so let him lead his life the way he wants. How long will you continue as his guide? Just inform his parents & let him be", Jyotika answered looking intently into Rajeev's eyes. Just as he was about to answer, Akhil walked into the canteen and stood still for a moment when he saw Rajeev with Jyotika. "Come and join us for coffee", Rajeev offered. "No, Sahil is waiting for me downstairs. Just came here to grab a drink", Akhil replied without looking at his friend and walked away immediately.

"I love this place, the only peaceful spot in the entire campus", Jyotika said. "Hmm, very true, I am desperately in need of some peace & quiet", Rajeev answered with a worried look. "In that case, let's walk to your favourite haunt in Kidwai Nagar. You can have all the peace that you want while I will get some fresh air", Jyotika said with a smile.

"This place is so quiet, I can sit here all day without a second thought", she said the moment they found a nice spot to sit at one end of the park. "You will get bored after spending a few days here. Besides, why does a beautiful girl like you need so much solitude"? Rajeev asked with a smile. "When one doesn't get good company what other options are left"? She questioned.

"Hmm, reading good books, going out on long walks, doing social work, falling in love", Rajeev listed a few options. "The last one seems good for you. Give it a try", Jyotika answered with a smile. "Let's go. It's getting dark. Need to devote some time for studies as well", Rajeev suggested. "Thanks for your company. And by the way, try to devote some time for yourself too. How long will you continue trying to reform someone? I don't think it will yield the desired result", Jyotika said as she slowly made her way into the hostel.

Rajeev reached the lobby of his hostel & sat down on the sofa. The words spoken by Jyotika made him feel uneasy. He was unsure about his next step. He got up and went to his room and switched on the light. Although he wanted to study, his mind was too pre-occupied with other thoughts. He closed his eyes, let his thoughts wander and before long he was fast asleep.

The sound of someone closing a suitcase made him wake up with a start. "Why are you packing your suitcase"? Rajeev asked upon seeing Akhil hurriedly lock the suitcase. "I am going with Mandeep to Amritsar tonight. His elder sister is getting engaged day after tomorrow", Akhil answered without looking at Rajeev.

"Wait! You can't leave just like that. Did you inform your family"? Rajeev asked trying to stop Akhil from leaving the room. "Stop interfering in my affairs, will you", Akhil hissed angrily pushing his friend to one side as he made his way to a cab parked outside. Rajeev stood there speechless. He did not realise then that this was going to be his last conversation with his friend.

CHAPTER-36

"Rajeev bhaiya, please open the door. I have come to take you to Lajpat Nagar", someone screamed while banging continuously on the door. Rajeev looked at the wall clock, it was 4.30 am. He hurriedly put on his jacket even as he rushed outside to open the door.

Before he could say anything, Ankit, who was Mandeep's classmate grabbed his hand & requested him to accompany him to his place. "Tell me what is wrong"? Rajeev asked Ankit. "I am afraid there is some terrible news. I got a call from Mandeep's sister that he was involved in a terrible bike accident in Moga. And .....' Ankit almost choked as he made a vain attempt to fight back his tears. "What? Please tell me", Rajeev begged as he collapsed on the floor.

"Mandeep and Akhil bhaiya are no more. They were crushed under the wheels of a dumper truck", Ankit somehow answered in a barely audible voice. Rajeev got up with some effort, dressed in a jiffy & accompanied Ankit. Not a word was uttered until he reached the apartment. Barring Kamaljeet & Santonu, almost everyone Rajeev knew had already gathered there. Someone had already informed the college authorities. All were waiting for Rajeev's arrival so that the news could be conveyed to Akhil's family.

With trembling hands, Rajeev dialled Mr. Gupta's number. "Rajeev what happened? Why did you call me so early? Are you guys in some trouble"? Mr. Gupta asked. "Things have gone horribly wrong, uncle. Akhil is no more. Please come at once", Rajeev answered barely able to retain his composure. There was no response from the other side as he could hear a loud thud probably caused by the phone slipping out of Mr. Gupta's hand & hitting the floor.

CHAPTER-37

Rajeev wiped off the tears from his swollen eyes as he and his friends waited outside the airport for Mr. Gupta's arrival. His flight touched down on time & as he approached none dared to greet him. Sahil looked at Rajeev & gave him a nudge but he was too scared to even look at Mr. Gupta who had concealed his bloodshot eyes behind dark glasses. Sahil and Arijit moved forward with folded hands and greeted him after introducing themselves. Without delay, they got into two taxis and headed straight to Amrit Nagar. Not a single word was uttered by anyone during the trip. Rajeev was the first to get down as he led the way to the apartment. Mr. Gupta followed slowly. Rajeev led him straight to the room which was occupied by Akhil. Rajeev had already packed Akhil's belongings neatly in order to ensure that Mr. Gupta faced no trouble. He motioned towards the chair and requested him to sit.

As he was about to leave the room to get a cup of tea for Mr. Gupta, he motioned Rajeev to sit. Rajeev froze in his tracks for some time and sat down with a downcast countenance. "How did that happen? Did I not tell you both to take care of each other when you left Guwahati? Did I not tell you not to allow my son out of your sights and yet you allowed him to travel all the way to Amritsar", Mr. Gupta reprimanded Rajeev. "Uncle, I tried to stop him but he wouldn't listen to me. I told him to inform at home before leaving but it now appears to me that he lied to me", Rajeev answered.

"No, he didn't inform us. And if he had refused to listen to you, then why didn't you call me"? Mr. Gupta asked looking up at Rajeev with his swollen red eyes. "Uncle, please don't misunderstand me. I tried hard to stop him but he got so angry that he almost wanted to hit me. Punish me if you want to but trust me when I say that I never forgot the promise I made to you. Although I admit I should have called you when I came to know of his plan to go this trip", Rajeev said even as he knelt down with folded hands and broke down in tears.

"Rajeev, I won't be able to forgive you for this. You have let me down badly", Mr Gupta said. "Pack his books in a suitcase and give it to me. Later on, if you get time please distribute his clothes and other belongings to the needy people that you see sitting in front of the temples", Mr Gupta said as he regained his composure. "A few of my relatives have gone to bring his body to Delhi. I shall leave tomorrow afternoon to Guwahati with them. You can accompany me if you want to. I am sure you want to be part of Akhil's last journey", Mr. Gupta added. Rajeev nodded in acknowledgement. "Okay, I will arrange your tickets. Just let me know when you want to return from Guwahati"? Mr Gupta asked. "I want to return the next day. Do you need anything"? Rajeev asked. "No, just leave me alone for some time. I will inform you if I require anything", Mr Gupta said.

CHAPTER-38

"Uncle, I have brought tea and some biscuits for you", Rajeev said. "Please order four chapattis & some boiled sabji for me for dinner. And please be ready by 1 pm tomorrow", Mr Gupta said. "Sure", Rajeev acknowledged and left the room.

Rajeev checked the time. It was 12.30 pm. He put on his shoes and knocked on the door. "Uncle, I have brought tea for you", Rajeev said. "Come in", Mr. Gupta responded. Rajeev went inside & placed the cup and a plate containing some bread slices on the table. Exactly at 1 pm, Mr. Gupta came out from the room with his luggage & looked at Rajeev who nodded and got up. Santonu and Kamaljeet accompanied them with a few others.

Rajeev turned his face towards the window as he wanted to avoid looking at Mr. Gupta. Memories of the time spent with Akhil made his eyes moist. "Have a safe journey", Santonu and the rest of the guys said as they helped Mr. Gupta to carry the luggage till the entry gate. As Rajeev bid goodbye to them & went towards the counter for check-in, he could see Akhil's maternal uncle and two other guys approach them. Mr. Gupta embraced him and broke down. Rajeev turned away from them & pretended not to look.

After completing the formalities, all of them settled down in a quiet corner of the departure lounge. Akhil's maternal uncle whose name was Suresh informed Mr. Gupta that he had completed all formalities like getting the body embalmed as well as collecting the necessary certificates from the hospital and the government authorities and handed over the documents to him.

The flight to Guwahati was uneventful. None uttered

a word. Mr. Gupta leaned on Suresh Ji's arm for support as they walked together towards the exit where Akhil's mother, his siblings & a host of other relatives were waiting. As they got ready to take the body home, Rajeev could hardly bear to stand and witness the sight of Akhil's mom and other relatives wailing in grief. It was not a sight for the faint-hearted. It was in moments like these that Rajeev wished the ground beneath would swallow him up.

As the procession reached Akhil's home, Rajeev could see his mom & dad waiting at one end of the sprawling verandah. He went straight to them. The reassuring feeling of his dad's embrace gave a lot of comfort to his grieving heart. After spending some time with Akhil's family, the Arora's left for their home.

CHAPTER-39

The cremation ceremony was well-attended. A sea of white congregated on the occasion as Mr. Gupta lit the funeral pyre. Mr. Arora and Suresh Ji stood holding Mr. Gupta as he almost collapsed with grief when he saw the flames engulf what remained of his son. Rajeev stood silently and watched from a distance. The sight of Akhil's body bearing severe wounds & injury marks almost made him pass out. He closed his eyes and prayed for everything to get over quickly.

As they made their way out of the cremation ground, Mr. Gupta motioned towards Rajeev as if he wanted to have a word with him. Rajeev approached him with fear writ large on his face. "Why didn't you stop him that night, Rajeev? Why didn't you"? Mr. Gupta asked. "I tried Uncle but he wouldn't listen", Rajeev whispered in between sobs. Mr. Gupta moved ahead with his family and relatives leaving Rajeev behind. There was no contact between the two families after that day.

Rajeev returned to Delhi the next day. He decided to immerse himself in his studies to forget the vacuum left behind by the demise of his friend. He was sitting alone in a corner of the canteen when Sahil saw him. "Hey Rajeev, when did you return"? He asked. "Just about a couple of hours ago", he replied. "Don't feel like attending classes for today", Rajeev continued. "It's alright. Take your time", Sahil said even as he ordered two cups of tea.

Rajeev went downstairs with Sahil. Santonu, Arijit & Kamaljeet were sitting on a bench in the park adjacent Chawla Ji's shop. Rajeev went in to meet them. "Hey Rajeev, we were expecting you. Did you attend the cremation ceremony"? Santonu asked. "I did", Rajeev nodded. "We were discussing something important and want to know your opinion", Kamaljeet said. "Santonu and I don't feel like staying in Amrit Nagar anymore. We have found a good place in Masjid Moth & want to shift there in a week", he continued.

Rajeev nodded in approval. Even he felt that moving to a new place will help him to let go of the painful memories. He accompanied the others to check out the new place. It was a new building bang opposite Harish departmental store. Rajeev liked the location & the freshly painted interiors of the apartment. While walking downstairs, they met Girish, the owner.

Santonu immediately handed him a token advance and confirmed that they will shift next week. Girish nodded and told them to collect the key from Ramphal, the caretaker.

CHAPTER-40

Rajeev was beginning to enjoy his stay at Ramakrishna apartments, his new address. The company of his friends helped him to tide over the crisis of losing his friend.

"Hello Rajeev, heard that you guys have shifted to a new apartment"? Jyotika asked. "Yes, we have", he replied. "What are you doing after class today"? She asked. "Well, just the usual stuff that I am used to. Eat, sleep and study", Rajeev replied. "Please accompany me to Kidwai Nagar in that case. Let's spend some time in the park", she replied.

Later in the evening, as they walked towards the park, Jyotika sensed that Rajeev was keeping unusually quiet. "You miss your friend a lot, don't you"? She asked. "Yes, I do but am trying to move on", he replied. "That's the spirit. I feel that you should not retreat into a shell. Share your thoughts with someone you trust. You will feel better", she suggested. "Hmm, that's a great idea. But whom do I trust? That is the dilemma", Rajeev answered. "You can share with me. I assure you that I won't share your secrets with anyone", she answered with a smile. "Let's see if I can really trust you. I don't usually trust anyone so easily", Rajeev said. "Take your time. I am not going anywhere", she replied.

Rajeev thanked Jyotika on their way back. "See, didn't I tell you that a long leisurely walk with me will do you a lot of good", Jyotika replied smilingly. "I agree I think we should make it a regular affair", Rajeev added. Ramphal was waiting for Rajeev in the balcony. "Bhaiya I hope you aren't facing any problem here", he asked when he saw Rajeev approaching. "Thankfully no", Rajeev answered. "Bhaiya, every new tenant gives me some baksheesh when they move in", Ramphal explained scratching his head. Rajeev too out a hundred rupee note and handed it to Ramphal. "Do let me know if you need any kind of help", Ramphal said before leaving.

"Rajeev what are you planning to do during the end semester break"? Santonu asked during dinner. "No major plans as of now", Rajeev replied. "Well, I and Kamaljeet are going home", Santonu replied.

CHAPTER-41

Attendance was very thin when Rajeev entered the class the next day. Most of his classmates were already in the holiday mood. Arvind and Aman Sir had just finished handing out the answer scripts to the class. As they day progressed, all the faculty members finished handing over the answer scripts back to the students.

"Let's have some celebration tonight. We can invite Arijit and a few other guys for dinner", Santonu suggested. "Why not", Kamaljeet agreed. "We will cook our own food this time", Rajeev said. It was around 9.30 when the boys finished the chores in the kitchen. The boys decided to have their food on the rooftop & all of them proceeded with their plates and a carpet to sit on. "Rajeev, why aren't you eating anything"? Santonu asked. "I know what you are thinking about. But there is no point feeling sad. Destiny plays a big part in our lives so we have to accept that fact. All we can do is pray for the departed soul. I am sure he is in a much better place than us", Kamaljeet said patting Rajeev on the back to cheer him up.

Post dinner, the boys sat down to play cards with some light music playing in the background. Rajeev sat on one side watching the others and before long he was fast asleep. He was awakened by the noise of someone closing the bathroom door. Santonu & Kamaljeet were getting ready to leave for the railway station. He quickly got up & asked if he could be of any help. "No we are almost done", Santonu smiled. "See you in a month's time", he continued.

All of them walked towards the auto stand a few hundred metres away. "You can stay with us for a few days if you want to. I am sure you will feel bored here all alone", Arijit offered. "Thanks guys, I will let you know", Rajeev replied even as he waved goodbye to his friends. He stopped to purchase a pouch of milk from Harish store on his way back.

CHAPTER-42

Rajeev headed to the library the next morning. As he was looking for some books on business communication, he felt a slight tap on his back. It was Jyotika. “I guess, you and the library are inseparable”, she said with a smile. “No I have nothing to do so I decided to come here”, Rajeev replied. “Same is the case with me. Let's sit here for some time”, she said. “How's your new apartment by the way”? She asked. “It's nice. All my friends like it”, he replied.

“Don't I fall in your category of friends Rajeev”? She asked. “Of course you do. Why did you ask”? He replied. “Because you haven't yet invited me to your place”, she said. “Oh, you can come any day”, Rajeev said in a rather unconvincing voice. “Is it? Then take me with you today”, she replied. “Sure thing, we can go post lunch”, he replied.

As they started walking, Rajeev was unsure how Girish bhaiya would react if he saw a lady accompanying him to his apartment. Thankfully, neither he nor Ramphal were around when he and Jyotika walked upstairs. Even then, Rajeev was visibly nervous and was sweating profusely. “What happened, Rajeev? Is something wrong with you”? Jyotika asked as she gently wiped away his sweat with her handkerchief. “No, no, I am alright”, he replied. “I guess you have never been all alone with a lady in a house. Don't worry. I am not here to make you anxious. Just relax”, she said, inching closer towards him.

“I will go and change”, Rajeev said and got up all of a sudden. As he was changing his shirt Jyotika who followed him to the other room was standing right in front of him and admiring his chest. Rajeev had been a regular at the gym while in Guwahati & had a nice, toned body. Jyotika came close to him once again, so close that he could feel her warm breath on his body. She ran a finger across his chest and smiled mischievously. Rajeev stood still as if in a daze. Never had he stood so close to a woman of such beauty. Her feminine grace had such an impact upon him that his lips moved forward and he planted a kiss on her forehead.

Anticipating another kiss, she started vigorously moving her left hand up and down his firm & sculpted chest even as she grabbed a pillow with her other hand almost burying her blood red finger nails in it. She lunged forward all of a sudden and made an attempt to get hold of his manhood. Rajeev could not resist a hard-on. He inched close to her and without warning grabbed her from behind. Jyotika let out a scream but Rajeev was in no mood to let go. He started squeezing her behind and rubbing his erect manhood against her body. He then slid his hands inside her panties after lifting her dress and thrust the middle finger of his right hand into her anal hole while he started vigorously rubbing and kneading her butts with the left hand.

She was pleasantly surprised and the savage assault unleashed on her made her feel so horny that she barely managed to bit her lower lip and suppress her desire to let out a scream. Rajeev now pulled down her panties to her ankles and made her sit on the bed and started fingering her pussy. She tried to resist but he grabbed her ankles firmly and thrust his tongue into her pussy. Jyotika who by now was in a highly aroused state tried to move away but Rajeev had her pinned down as his tongue went deeper and deeper inside her.

He released his grip on her ankles as some pre-cum started oozing out from her pussy. She covered her face with one hand and started moaning loudly even as she started pinching her nipples with the other. She could feel the love juices churning inside her. In the meantime, Rajeev took off his underwear and was standing completely naked in front of Jyotika who could not suppress a feeble smile on seeing him so well hung. He got going immediately to complete his unfinished task and removed her panties from her ankles ignoring her mock protests and the feeble resistance put up by her and unhooked her bra almost tearing it apart in the process.

He now shifted his attention to her juicy tits and started licking and squeezing them alternately. She drew her legs tightly around him and buried her blood red finger nails into his back. Rajeev by now was more like a volcano ready to erupt. He lifted her on his shoulders and placed her on the bed. Before Jyotika could even make out what was to follow Rajeev once again spread her legs wide and plunged his throbbing dick into her pussy. She winced in pain and tried to move away but he took no notice and instead increased his pace and started moving his dick back and forth into her pussy with renewed intensity. He now turned her around, and made her go down on her knees.

Jyotika, who by now was enjoying every moment of it, tried to play hard to get by trying to move away in order to take her pleasure level to a new high and resisting his moves but all this only made him want her all the more. He pinned her down hopelessly, grabbed her wrists tightly and plunged his manhood with all his might into her pussy from behind. 'Oh Rajeev, I never knew you could make love in this manner, you like my pussy don't you, I love your prick fitting tightly inside my pussy, fuck me baby, fuck real hard,fuck ,oh fuck,ummm, unmf, fill me with cum'. She started moaning when she could hold back no longer.

He could feel his balls tighten and the cum brewing inside him, as he took out his love tool and slid it into her anal hole with one mighty thrust. She let out a huge shriek but Rajeev was not done yet and with each thrust his dick moved deeper and deeper into her anal hole. He grabbed her tits from behind and started squeezing them violently while he kept on pounding her ass. She was hopelessly pinned down could sense the storm churning inside him while she could feel his balls tighten as they slapped against her butts with his every thrust. And then without warning, his grip on her wrists tightened even further, his seeds burst and he let loose a huge load of cum inside her.

Tired and drained Rajeev slumped next to a badly battered and almost breathless Jyotika. But he was not done yet; he got up after some time and now started fingering and teasing her pussy once again while holding her legs apart from each other. He increased the intensity and force while she moaned loudly and grabbed his face and tried to push it deeper and deeper into her womanhood. Her love juices started trickling down all over again, in small drops initially, but gradually the flow increased and then all of a sudden her nostrils flared up, her body started shaking & heaving violently as she let out a huge shriek and dug her nails deep into his back while letting loose her love juices which trickled out of her love hole and covered Rajeev's face. Tired and totally drained, both slumped to the floor and passed out.............

Rajeev was jolted out of his sleep all of a sudden by a sound close to his left ear. He looked around and picked up his mobile phone.

Jyotika had sent him a text message. "Thanks for your company and for making me feel so special. I really love you but I could not gather enough courage to confess my feelings for you. I was determined to declare my love for you today but I was not prepared for what transpired between us. Sorry, I left without informing you as I did not want you to feel awkward. I eagerly await your reply. Take care".

Rajeev remembered how Akhil desperately wanted to woo Jyotika. The fact that he just made wild, passionate love to her troubled him even more. He carelessly flung his mobile to one side and closed his eyes.

INTERLUDE

CHAPTER-43

"Why don't you shift to a one room apartment"? Kamaljeet asked. "I have postponed my plans to return to Delhi for the time being and Santonu called me up yesterday saying that he has decided to shift to Jamia Nagar with Sahil", he continued. "But when you left Delhi you told me that you will return after a month", Rajeev said. "I did, but things have changed now and my parents are planning to send me abroad for higher studies, Canada to be precise, and I have a relative here who has helped many job-seekers and students to travel abroad and I have to remain in Chandigarh to complete the formalities. Why don't you go back to Saxena's hostel? I am sure that old fellow would be happy to accommodate you", Kamaljeet said in a sarcastic tone. "Thanks for your advice but I hope you remember that before boarding the bus at the ISBT you told me that you would definitely return and in case you had to change plans you will transfer your share of the room rent to my account. Same was the case with Santonu", Rajeev said desperately trying to control his desire to yell at his friend. "I am sorry about that but I am afraid I won't be able to send you any money. If you don't mind, we will talk later, okay", Kamaljeet said and disconnected the call even before Rajeev could reply.

"Bhaiya, Girish sahab aap ko niche bula rahein hain", Ramphal called out after knocking on the door and went away without waiting for a reply. Rajeev put on a shirt lying on his bed and walked slowly towards the congested, dusty office of the landlord located in one corner of the basement. He paused just before entering the room and gathered his thoughts. By now, he had run out of excuses, his friends had deserted him and he had no money to pay the rent. “Hey come in, why are you standing outside”? Girish called out when he saw Rajeev standing at the door. Unsure of what to say, Rajeev walked slowly inside, his footsteps as uncertain as his thoughts were at that moment. “So are you going to pay the rent today? You promised to pay me within ten days but today is the last day of the month”, Girish said in a polite but firm tone. “Bhaiya, my room-mates have refused to send me money”, Rajeev said deciding to make a clean breast of everything. “Listen young man, I am least bothered about all these things as I don't know what went wrong between you and your friends. But considering the hopeless position that you have put yourself in I am giving you one week's time to arrange the money”. Girish said pointing a finger at Rajeev as if trying to emphasise his seriousness. “Thank you bhaiya, I won't take that long”, Rajeev said heaving a sigh of relief.

After coming out from the landlord's office Rajeev headed straight to Harish General Store to get some food items. Although the shop was located some distance away, he knew that the trouble was worth it as it was the only place where he could procure kitchen provisions on credit. “Rajeev how are you? If you want something decide quickly, I am about to leave”, Harish said. Rajeev took was what required and after noting it down on the register and signing it was about to leave when Harish motioned to him to wait. “I came to know from Ramphal that your room-mates have left without paying the rent.

Why don't you shift to some other place? You are putting too much strain on your dad. Don't mind yaar, but I think you don't need to stay in a three bedroom apartment just to prove a point to someone,” Harish said. Rajeev smiled feebly in response and left after thanking him. “Bhaiya there is a letter for you”, Ramphal called out from behind when he saw Rajeev near the gate. Without even looking at the envelope he carelessly folded it and put it inside his shirt pocket. Still sweating profusely after the long walk in the sweltering heat Rajeev switched on the fan, sat down on the chair and took out the envelope. It contained his MAT scorecard. The neat rows and columns containing the scaled scores set in a fluorescent green background looked impressive. Composite score was 576.50. "Nothing to write home about", he muttered under his breath as he flung it carelessly in the direction of his study-table. His cell-phone beeped. "Money transferred to your account at 12.45 pm, check and get back to me", was what his dad wrote in the SMS.

CHAPTER-44

As he dressed up again he felt relieved that finally he would be able to repay his debts. Not surprisingly, the walk from Masjid Moth to South Extension Part I market did not take him too long. The familiar face of the old man slowly counting the currency notes reminded him of the first time he walked into the bank three years ago. “How are you son? You look so thin, take good care of your health”, the cashier spoke as he handed Rajeev a bundle of crisp currency notes neatly placed between the pages of his passbook. “I am fine uncle”, Rajeev said even as he counted the money. Girish was having his lunch with his friends in his office when Rajeev walked up to him. “Bhaiya, here is the rent for two months”, Rajeev said even before Girish could speak. “I will vacate the apartment by the end of this month. Thanks a lot for being so kind to me”, Rajeev continued with a smile. “So you have finally decided to leave Delhi. Good for you, I guess. This place does not suit your health. I think you will be better off in your hometown”, Girish said. Rajeev unlocked the door of his apartment, switched on the fan and almost collapsed on his bed with exhaustion. His thoughts went back to the day he decided to come to Delhi. Tears welled up in his eyes and for the first time in his life he made no attempt to wipe them off. Life had treated him unkindly and he felt terribly lonely.

Rajeev was reminded of the day when his friend went away on a road trip to Amritsar with Mandeep paying scant attention to his objections. Akhil almost got involved in a fisticuff with Rajeev when he got angry at his numerous attempts to dissuade him. That was also the last time Rajeev saw his friend alive. A week later all that he saw was Akhil's injury-ridden, blood spattered body wrapped in a shroud being readied for one final journey before being consigned to flames. He still remembered how Akhil's dad sobbed uncontrollably staring almost in a motionless manner at the lifeless body of his son even as Rajeev watched helplessly, afraid to even lend him a supporting shoulder to lean upon. Rajeev had failed to keep his promise made to Akhil's dad of looking after him as his own brother and protecting him from harm. He watched from a safe distance, not because he feared that Akhil's dad would yell at him but because he feared of being labelled a failure. Very soon Akhil became a distant memory for everyone around him, an irrelevant speck in the distant horizon. But for him the memories of his friend would be impossible to erase and forget, Rajeev thought, desperately trying to fight back his tears. The time spent in the company of everyone at Saxena Ji's hostel, the sound of those ear-splitting farts that echoed the walls every time Dadaji went to the toilet, the evenings spent gossiping at the Park in Kidwai Nagar, the lovely and intimate moments spent with Shilpi & Jyotika all appeared frivolous now. Rajeev hated people who behaved like losers but now he was acting like one. He wondered what Jyotika thought about him. She must have labelled him as a coward & banished him from her mind.

CHAPTER-45

He was about to return home with failure writ large on his face. But what caused him even more agony was the huge financial burden that his dad had to bear to fund an unfulfilled dream. It was 5.30 in the evening. Without taking too long, he headed straight to AVS Tours and Travels as he knew well that he had only a week left to vacate the apartment and therefore had to book his train ticket at the earliest. "Sorry Sir, all trains to Guwahati are booked to capacity till the middle of next month", the ticketing executive said. "Please check again if any seats are available in two-tier or first class", Rajeev said with a worried look on his face. "I am sorry Sir", the executive answered after taking another look at the computer screen. "Why don't you take the early morning Air Sahara flight to Guwahati on the 30th"? The executive asked. "How much is the fare"? Rajeev asked.

"One way economy-class fare is Rupees 10,500", the lady said still looking intently at the figures displayed on the screen. "Thanks", Rajeev said as he walked out from the office after picking up a student air travel concession form lying on the table. After an early breakfast the next morning, Rajeev went to meet Prakash Srivastava. As he waited in the visitor's lounge, some familiar faces went past him. Some nodded their heads in his direction as if to acknowledge his presence while some others did not even bother looking at him. "After all, it is just a business for them. Those who have completed their studies would be making no further contributions towards their salaries by filling the coffers of the institute", Rajeev thought.

Exactly at 10.15 am Srivastava walked in and went straight into his cabin. As soon as Rajeev saw the peon come out after placing a pile of registers' on the CEO's desk he got up and went in after knocking on the door. “So what brings you here”? Srivastava asked. “I hope it is something important this time Rajeev. As you can see I am very busy today”, he spoke again pointing at the heap of files lying on his desk. “Sir, I am going back to Guwahati. Just need you signature on this form”, Rajeev replied as he placed the concession form in front of him. Srivastava signed at the marked places. “Thank you sir”, Rajeev said and without looking back walked out of the office building for the last time.

He now headed straight to the Travel agency. “Hello sir, please be seated”, the receptionist welcomed him. “Please book me a ticket in the 'J' Class latest by the 30th”, Rajeev said after handing over the form and his College Identity card. “You can come back after about forty-five minutes and collect your ticket. As such tickets are issued only by the airline office in Connaught Place, we are sending someone to collect it from them”, the lady said after handing him the cash receipt.

Finally, the day arrived when Rajeev had to leave. As the taxi made its way towards Ring Road, he cast a glance in the direction of Saxenaji's Guest House. “Things would have taken a very different turn had I listened to my dad's advice and not moved out from here”, he thought.

It was exactly 6 am and flight no S 2112 was ready for take-off. A sense of gloom enveloped the aura of a depressed Rajeev. The first rays of the sun which caressed through the window to fall on him made him only more agitated. He knew that there would be no immediate respite from the unhappy memories. Delhi delighted him only to disappoint in the end.

Epilogue I

ONE YEAR LATER

“How long will you just sit there running your fingers over that computer keyboard”? Mrs Arora growled. “You have already done enough damage to your dad's finances, how long do you want to continue in this manner”? She continued her tone almost resembling the roar of a lioness. Rajeev did not feel like answering back. Instead he walked to the front yard for a leisurely stroll and let his thoughts wander. He knew that he had lost the right to complain. Just then he heard the phone ring. “Hello, who is this”? He heard his mother answer the call. “Rajeev, a call for you from someone named Laskar”, his mother called out. Rajeev hurried inside wondering who the caller could be. “Hey Rajeev, this is Laskar from CABSFORD Public Relations”, the person at the other end spoke as soon as he sensed that someone had picked up the receiver. “You had submitted your CV at our office in response to our advertisement in the newspaper. We are conducting a written test next Sunday. Please reach our office at 10.00 am sharp”, he continued. 'Sure”, Rajeev said and disconnected the call after thanking him. “Now go and pick up those books lying on your table and start preparing seriously for that test. If you get that job I would still be able to tell our nosy neighbours that you are atleast doing something worthwhile after your return from Delhi”, Mrs Arora said.

“Please stop writing everyone”, Laskar called out as soon as the clock struck twelve noon. One by one all the candidates walked up to him and handed over their answer scripts. “The results will be out in a week's time”, he spoke again even as his wife who was standing next to him handed each one of them a chocolate bar and a glass of fruit juice.

Rajeev had done well in the test and was eagerly waiting for the interview call. But when he did not get a call till late afternoon on the tenth day after the test he began to lose hope. Just then, the phone rang. Rajeev ran and picked up the receiver as if his very life depended on the phone call. “Hello Rajeev, this is Laskar once again. Sorry for the delay. I had to go to Imphal to organise a press meet for a major client. You have done well in the test and I want you to come down for an interview tomorrow at 2 in the afternoon”. “Ok sir”, Rajeev replied. This was surely an opportunity that he did not want to miss.

He reached the office well ahead of time and after exchanging pleasantries with two other candidates sat down and waited for his turn. From the corner where he was seated, he could see Laskar dressed in an immaculate black suit, white shirt and matching tie interviewing a smart looking female candidate. “So are you from Guwahati”? The man sitting next to him asked politely. “Yes”, Rajeev replied. “By the way, I am Rupam Phukan”; the other man said extending his hand in Rajeev's direction. “I am Rajeev Arora”, he said and shook his hand.

After some time, the female candidate walked out from the cabin and Rajeev, enchanted by the delightful fragrance that wafted into the room as she walked past craned his neck and looked in her direction. But with graceful yet swift steps she was out of sight even before he could catch a glimpse of her face. “Is Rajiv here”? The office peon called out. Rajeev stood up, gathered his thoughts and walked confidently towards the cabin flanked by the peon. “Hello Rajeev”, Laskar greeted him cheerfully. Rajeev shook hands with him and scanned the room. There were two more members in the interview panel, Mrs Laskar and a young woman who was probably only a couple of years older than him. “Please have a seat”, the young woman said. Rajeev nodded politely and sat down in the only vacant chair in the room. “So you have done BBA from an institute in New-Delhi, what made you come back to Guwahati”? Laskar enquired. “I could not get into a good institute for further studies as I did not do well in the entrance exams and I also had some health related issues”, Rajeev replied honestly. “Are you okay now”? Laskar asked with a frown on his face even as he ran a finger through his thick beard. “I had a bout of typhoid but I am well now”, Rajeev replied. “Since you have done well in the test we want you to join our firm from next month”, Laskar said and handed him a letter. “Please go through and if the terms are acceptable to you then we can proceed further. Since ours is a small firm we would only be able to offer you a modest salary but we are confident that things will improve sooner than later”, he continued. Rajeev went through the details carefully and signed at the places marked for him. “Thanks Rajeev, here's your letter of appointment. You can join us from next Monday”, Laskar said. Rajeev got up thanked everyone present in the cabin and walked out of the office.

One week into his job, Rajeev was enjoying every moment of it. During the lunch break he logged on to face book and posted the following status update- “Time to move on in life. I have somehow managed to weather the storm. Life is back on track. But my best is yet to come”. Rajeev's mood was upbeat. And he felt that the time was ripe for him to let the world know.

Epilogue II

SIX YEARS LATER

"Would you like to have a cup of tea"? The housekeeper asked. "No, I will have my lunch a bit early today. You may have a cup if you feel like. Also please ask the physiotherapist and the nurse if they need anything", Rajeev said and went back to his room. He began pacing up & down his room. If things don't go his way once again, he was unsure what he would do next.

His cell phone beeped. It was an SMS from his cousin.

"Good morning brother. How are you doing? I think the results will be declared today. I will call you as soon as I get to know anything more."

"Thanks", Rajeev messaged back. He was in no mood to type out a long message.

9.30 pm

"Your mother's health is deteriorating with each passing day. If it continues, I am afraid she won't be around for too long", Mr Arora said. "What happened? Why are you not having your dinner? Don't you like the food"? Mr Arora asked. "No Dad. There is nothing wrong with the food. I am not hungry, that's all", Rajeev replied, the tension and uneasiness evident in his voice.

"Come on son, tell me what is bothering you so much", Mr Arora asked again with a look of concern on his face. "It's nothing Dad. I am absolutely fine", Rajeev replied. Rajeev's cell phone beeped once again.

"Congratulations brother! You have cleared the entrance. I just checked the results", wrote his cousin.

Rajeev almost ran to his room and started typing furiously on his computer. The wait for the page to be displayed seemed like eternity. "Yes, I have made it", Rajeev exclaimed in excitement. "Dad, I am joining IITG soon", Rajeev declared. "That's great. Well done son", Mr Arora said patting his son's back.

October 29, 2011

"Hello son! Hope you are attending classes attentively. If you can make some time, please come & see your mom once. She is in the ICU", Mr Arora said in a voice almost choking with emotion. "Okay Dad. I will be there in a couple of hours", Rajeev said. "Visiting hours is from 1pm to 2 pm so be on time", Mr Arora said and disconnected the call.

As Rajeev walked past the lobby of the hospital, he could feel his heart beat quicken. He couldn't imagine his mother lying on a hospital bed, unable to move, being tube fed. He took a deep breath before going up the final flight of stairs to the ICU block. He tried to put up a brave face when he saw his father as he had always done during the last couple of years. But he failed miserably this time. As he neared him, Rajeev could feel the tears swell up in his eyes. He made no attempt to wipe them off. Instead, he embraced his dad & let the tears flow.

November 01, 2011

Rajeev is rudely jolted up from his sleep at 5.30 am by a loud knock on his door. He got up from his bed even as the knocking sound grew louder by the second. Standing outside was his maternal uncle, with swollen eyes & tears running down his face.

"Your mother is no more. Get ready as quickly as you can", he said to Rajeev. Rajeev did not know what to say. He stood still for a while, as if in a daze, before regaining his composure.

June 08, 2013

"Dear students, I welcome you all to the 15th Convocation Ceremony of IIT, Guwahati. We will start the proceedings in a short while from now. I request you all to maintain silence and switch off your mobiles till the ceremony is over. Thank you", the announcer said & left the dais.

"Rajeev, your seat is right next to me. Romen Ningthoujam called out waving his arm. "Why are you late"? Romen asked as soon as Rajeev had taken his seat. "Sorry yaar, I woke up late. Please accept my apologies", Rajeev said.

After the ceremony got over, Rajeev had his lunch and then proceeded to return his robe before heading straight to the designated lecture hall to collect his mark sheet. After waiting for sometime, the institute staff came & called out the names of the assembled students one by one.

"What happened, Rajeev Da? Why are you sitting all alone at the back? Is something worrying you"? Parag Deka Baruah asked. "No, it's okay. The thought of leaving this institute and you guys is making me feel sad", Rajeev replied.

Rajeev felt relieved that he could give a convincing reply. But what he said was far from the truth. Yes, something was bothering him at that moment. But he chose to keep it to himself and suffer silently. He had achieved something big in life on that day but strangely enough, found no reason to celebrate. He was missing that one person in his life who always prayed to God earnestly for his success, well-being and happiness while she was alive. How proud she would have been to know that her son had finally done something noteworthy in life. He held his certificate and mark sheet close to his chest and walked away from the class-room, silently, unnoticed. His eyes became moist and tear drops started trickling down his face as he continued his walk towards the hostel.

What really mattered to him was that his long suppressed sorrows had finally found an outlet that provided some relief to his weary heart. "Success had come to him finally, or was it success at all", Rajeev wondered. After all, his mother passed away, dejected and heart-broken at not being able to see her only son do well in life.

www.ingramcontent.com/pod-product-compliance
Ingram Content Group UK Ltd.
Pitfield, Milton Keynes, MK11 3LW, UK
UKHW041956190726
13854UKWH00005B/2010